THE INNOCENT

In 1948, Aleksandr, a major in the MGB
— forerunner of the KGB — is sent to a
psychiatric clinic in the Ural mountains to
investigate a patient, Second World War
veteran Anatoly Yudin — a man long
presumed dead . . . It's 1972, the year of
Nixon's visit to Moscow; the Munich
Olympics and their hostage crisis — the
Cold War is entering détente, and the
values that shaped Aleksandr's life become
uncertain. Haunted by the past, his
Stalinist faith again under threat, he
interrogates his memories of the Yudin
case, and tries to trace its effects on
himself, and on those he loved most.

DAVID SZALAY

◆

THE INNOCENT

Complete and Unabridged

ULVERSCROFT
Leicester

First published in Great Britain in 2009 by
Jonathan Cape
The Random House Group Limited
London

First Large Print Edition
published 2010
by arrangement with
The Random House Group Limited
London

British Library CIP Data

Szalay, David.
   The innocent.
   1. Intelligence officers- -Russia (Federation)- -Fiction.
   2. Communism- -Russia (Federation)- -Fiction.
   3. Psychiatric hospital patients- -Russia (Federation)- -
   Fiction. 4. Russia (Federation)- -Social conditions- -
   Fiction. 5. Large type books.
   I. Title
   823.9′2–dc22

   ISBN 978–1–44480–102–6

For my parents

Chronology

February 1917   February Revolution, abdication of tsar, formation of Provisional Government

October 1917   October Revolution; Lenin overthrows Provisional Government and establishes Soviet power

1919–21   Civil War and Allied intervention

1921   Famine and introduction of New Economic Policy (NEP), which restores private property and free-market mechanisms to much of the economy

1924   Death of Lenin

1929   'Stalin Revolution'. End of NEP, start of first industrial Five Year Plan and collectivisation of agriculture

December 1934	Murder of Sergei Mironovich Kirov, a member of the Politburo, in Leningrad
1937	'Great Purge'
June 1941	Nazi Germany invades the Soviet Union
1941–45	'Great Patriotic War'
March 1953	Death of Stalin
September 1953	Khrushchev takes over as First Secretary
February 1956	Khrushchev makes 'Secret Speech', in which he denounces Stalin, to Twentieth Party Congress; process of 'de-Stalinisation' starts
October 1964	Khrushchev succeeded by Brezhnev as First Secretary and Kosygin as Premier
1968	Richard Nixon elected President of USA
May 1972	Nixon visits Soviet Union
July–September 1972	Bobby Fischer of the USA and Boris Spassky of the USSR contest World Chess

Championship in Reykjavik

August–Sept. 1972   Olympic Games in Munich

October 1972   US-Soviet Trade Agreement signed; Brezhnev to visit USA in 1973

Note

The Soviet Union was divided into Republics (e.g. Russia, Ukraine, Georgia, Kazakhstan) which were further divided into regions. The Russian word for these regions is *oblast*. As with the USSR as a whole, each *oblast* had parallel state and party bureaucracies — the *obkom* was the highest party body in the *oblast*, the *oblispolkom* its state equivalent — and as in the USSR as a whole, the party always had the final word. As Stephen Kotkin puts it, 'Both parts of the party-state were functional, but their functions were different: whereas the state's role was defined in terms of competent technical and economic administration, the party's was defined in terms of ideological and political guidance. Such a bifurcated political system, with the party analogous to a church, resembled a kind of theocracy.'[1] Thus, while day-to-day administration was handled by state institutions, the first secretary of the *obkom* was the most

---

[1] Stephen Kotkin, *Magnetic Mountain*: Stalinism as a **Civilisation** (University of California Press 1995)

powerful individual in the *oblast*. Much of this power was exercised through the *nomenklatura*, a list of senior positions — in all walks of life, including the *oblispolkom* — which were filled only with *obkom* nominees.

Technically part of the state bureaucracy, the state security police was in fact more or less independent, part of a separate and parallel structure, with the Ministry of State Security in Moscow at its summit. It was formed in 1917 and was known as the Cheka, the 'All-Russian Extraordinary Commission for Combating Counter-Revolution, Profiteering and Sabotage'. Throughout the Soviet period, state security officers were popularly known as 'Chekists'. The institution itself was known by an ever-shifting series of acronyms. Put simply, the Cheka became the GPU (State Political Directorate) in 1922, the OGPU (Unified State Political Directorate) in 1923, the NKVD (People's Commissariat of Internal Affairs) in 1934, the MGB (Ministry of State Security) in 1946 and the KGB (State Security Committee) in 1954.

1

When he wakes it is dark. He fell asleep listening to the birds twittering in the cherry tree outside until their twitters were the only thing he was aware of. When he was no longer aware even of them, he dreamed of Metelyev Log. Exactly what, he does not know, but for a few minutes, when he wakes, he has a very strong sense of the place.

Still lying on the sofa in the dark, he sees that the sense he has is not so much of the place as of himself as he was then, when he was there, in 1948. The place, of course, is part of that — so much so that he feels it would be possible to undertake some sort of interrogation of it, that it would have something to say to him about himself, as he was then.

Standing slowly, he turns on the overhead light, then the record player — the greenish dials spring to life with a soft thump — and puts on the LP of Rikhter playing Bach. Some preludes and fugues from the *Well-tempered Clavier*. Having such strong associations with Metelyev Log, the music hugely intensifies the sense he woke up with, which had been

1

starting to dissipate in the warm, 1972 night air. After a few moments of almost hallucinatory evocation, however, the effect turns sad. The music, while evoking a place and a time — they seem the same thing — with extreme intensity, also emphasises distance, and so nostalgic indulgence turns to sadder appraisal. He thinks of the people. Of Mikhail Naumovich Lozovsky, who was arrested in the summer of 1948.

Of his wife, Nadezhda.

2

The 1930s were a period of feverish activity, and stupendous progress was made in a short time. A thousand important projects seemed to be proceeding all at once. I started the decade as a student at the Feliks Dzerzhinsky OGPU Higher School in Moscow. It was a period of immense excitement. We felt like apostles, prepared to sacrifice everything in the name of the monumental struggle in which we were engaged. The making of Communism was something sacred to us. I find myself using Christian language, and I suspect that Christianity was in part the muddled response of a pre-scientific age to some of the same things that Marxism is a scientific response to — the need to make sense of our existence, and the need for hope. So it seems natural to use the same sort of language. The language of faith. The language of a new heaven, and a new earth. Because that was what we thought we were making — a new heaven, and a new earth. As Blok put it, 'Everything had to be new, so that our false, filthy, tedious, hideous life was transformed into a just, pure, merry life.' That, for us, was the spirit of the 1930s.

The forties were more sombre. There was the war. And after the war, the exhausted peace. It was less easy, then, to have faith that we were making a new heaven and a new earth. I think, for all of us, there were, in the late forties, moments of doubt.

★ ★ ★

The place was known as Metelyev Log. It was not a village, or a settlement of any sort, just an old summer palace out in the sticks, then a sort of hospital. It was not far from Sverdlovsk. Nevertheless, it took a few hours to get there. The train puffed up a little, mountainous spur into the forest. The nameless little stations, with their slippery log platforms, were empty. It was raining. I remember thinking: what a place to hide, up here in this silent forest, far away from everything.

I was there to speak to one of the inmates, Anatoly Lvovich Yudin. It was too late to see him on the night I arrived. I stayed with Lozovsky, the director of the hospital, and his wife. Lozovsky was, or had been, one of the stars of Soviet science. He was then in his mid-forties, his reddish hair starting to turn grey. He warned me that we were 'in the country'. 'Oh, I like that,' I said. 'Don't worry. I like the country.' However, my shoes were not

4

suitable for the short walk to his house, which seemed to be in the forest somewhere.

Though he warned me that Yudin had severe mental and physical disabilities, he was not very specific. He said it would be easier to explain once I had met him. The meeting took place the next morning in his office, a large, plain room, the windows of which overlooked what was once perhaps a lawn, now more of a meadow, sloping down to the shore of a lake. In fact, Yudin was an ordinary-looking man. I knew him immediately from photographs I had seen, though when I met him his head was shaved, like a prisoner's. The only sign that there was perhaps something wrong was the fact that, with a hand on his elbow, a pretty, dark-haired young woman seemed to be steering him into the room. Was he blind? No — he saw me and smiled. There was, however, something strange about this smile.

Lozovsky shut the door.

'This is Doctor Anichkova,' he said, introducing the young woman. 'And this is . . . '

Though he was still smiling, Yudin was obviously frightened. 'Hello,' I said, and held out my hand. 'Anatoly Yudin?' And then the first strange thing happened. He hesitated for a moment, tried to take my hand — and missed it. That he was able to see it was obvious. His eyes were fixed on it purposefully.

Nevertheless, his own hand kept squeezing empty air. Puzzled, I took it for a moment. 'Are you Anatoly Yudin?' I said.

When he said nothing, just smiled steadily in the same frightened, unsettling way, I looked at Lozovsky, who also said nothing. 'Could you tell me your name?' I said to Yudin. At first he did not seem to understand. Then, when I asked a second time, speaking very slowly, he said, 'Okay, yes,' with a serious nod. He did not, however, tell me his name. 'Your name,' I said. 'What is it?'

He seemed perplexed — 'I . . . I . . . '

'What's your name?'

'It's . . . ' He was no longer smiling — his expression was painful with effort. He shook his head.

'Is it Anatoly Yudin?'

'Anatoly Yudin,' he said, though seemingly without understanding what the words were.

Nevertheless, I pressed on. I said, 'Where are you from?'

For a long time Yudin seemed to think about this. Eventually he shook his head, as if to say, 'Tell me. I don't know.'

'Where are you from?' I said. 'Are you from Sverdlovsk?' He nodded, though he did not seem to know what I was talking about. I patted him on the shoulder. 'It's okay,' I said. 'Let's sit down.' Sitting was not easy for him.

Anichkova had to help him, steady him, steer him into the seat. In some ways he seemed like someone who was extremely drunk. When we were sitting I said, 'How long have you been here? Do you know how long you've been here?'

'I . . . I . . . don't . . . ' He shook his head.

We sat in silence. Then I said, 'You've been here since January forty-four.' Something in this seemed vaguely familiar to him. His expression sharpened slightly. Encouraged, I said, 'You've been here since January forty — '

And suddenly, startling me, he said, 'January februarymarchaprilmay.' He smiled. He seemed pleased with himself.

Seeing that I was at a loss, Lozovsky intervened and suggested that Anichkova take Yudin out, which, with some difficulty, she did.

When they had left, Lozovsky tried to explain the situation to me. 'You probably don't appreciate,' he said, 'the extent to which your mind creates the sense of order, stability and meaning that you have about the world around you. I'm not talking about anything philosophical here. Just the fact that when you see things, you know what they are, and where they are. You know what a pencil is when you see it. A letter opener, you know what it is. Things make sense. Spatially — as simple as that. The pencil is on the desk. To the left of it

7

is the ashtray. It's all very easy to understand, isn't it? In fact, it's so easy to understand that it seems strange to talk about 'understanding' at all. You might wonder: how is it possible not to understand? We seem to be talking about intrinsic properties of things we perceive. In perceiving them, we seem totally passive. This isn't so however. And one of the reasons we know it isn't, is that Anatoly Lvovich does not understand.' He spoke fluently, impersonally, as if to a lecture hall full of students, with a sort of smile in his grey eyes. 'So,' he said, 'what doesn't he understand? Two things, mainly. First, physical space. And second, language. He suffers from aphasia — the loss of the ability to use and understand language.'

He said that Yudin had been shot in the head, in 1942. That he had survived such an injury was improbable. He had been operated on, and Lozovsky showed me the original surgeon's report. 'Essentially,' he said, summarising its technicalities, 'he had the back of his head blown off.' He put his hand on the upper part of his own head, where the hair was thinning. 'Here.' Yudin's situation was interesting, he said, because of the severity of the injury to one part of the brain, while leaving all other parts intact — 'which is obviously useful from the point of view of my studies, since what I study is how damage to different parts of the brain affects a person's ability to think, speak and understand the speech of others.' He said that in Yudin's case the injured part had several important functions. Notably, taking sensory information and forming it into a meaningful whole, and playing an essential, if little understood, part in the use of language. Hence Yudin's problems, which Lozovsky said were the normal effects of an injury like his. 'Plus amnesia, of course. When I first knew him, he had no memory. Nothing at all. And I mean nothing at all. Not a single word. Then, after a few months, there was some improvement. His own name. His sisters' names. Some things from his childhood. That's what you'd expect. His short-term memory's very poor though. More or less non-existent.'

'He didn't seem to know his own name just now,' I said.

Lozovsky smiled. 'No. Sometimes he knows it, sometimes he doesn't. It's like that with everything.'

'He's never had any visitors?'

'No.'

'And no letters?'

'No.'

'The months,' I said. 'He could go through the months. He seemed to be able to do it easily, fluently.'

'Yes.' Lozovsky seemed to think for a

moment. 'That's something else,' he said.

'Is it? What?'

'Well . . . When we learn things early in life, by saying them over and over — sequences especially, like the months — we develop what I would describe as a 'muscle memory' of them. So he still has that, but it's only a kinetic motor function, a 'muscle memory'. That's why he still has it. He doesn't understand what he's saying.'

I had lunch with Lozovsky and some of the other hospital staff. Later I said to him, 'Is it possible that it's all some kind of act?'

He laughed. 'No, of course not.' I did not say anything — I wanted to let him think about it some more. 'Of course not.' Still I said nothing. 'It's not possible.'

'Why not?'

'His injuries.'

'Yes?'

'Anyone with those injuries would show the symptoms he shows. It's not possible that they wouldn't.'

'But how can you be sure about the injuries?' I said. 'Can you be sure about them by looking at his head now?' He said something about the surgeon's report. 'The surgeon's report could be forged,' I suggested.

He laughed again. 'Do you think it's forged?' he asked.

10

'I don't know,' I said. 'I don't know for a fact that it isn't. Let's say,' I went on, 'for the sake of argument, that it is. Let's look at his behaviour — could that be . . . '

'An act? No . . . '

'Why not?'

'Are you really suggesting,' he said, 'that for the past four years, and more, he has spent every single day pretending to be in the state you've seen?'

'I'm not suggesting anything,' I said. 'I'm wondering if it's possible.'

'I don't think it is possible.'

'Why not?'

'Because the pattern of his symptoms is exactly what we'd expect from someone with the injuries described in the report! I don't think someone who wasn't a neuropsychologist, an expert, would know what that was. We're not stupid, you know. If his behaviour was full of anomalies we'd have been suspicious ourselves. And what would be the point?' he said impatiently. 'What would be the point of it?' He stubbed out his papirosa. 'It's silly.'

I stood up and went to the window while he watched me nervously. It did seem silly. Outside, everything was misty, wet. Primeval forest sinking into muddy twilight. It was time for me to leave, and I was looking forward to leaving. There was only one more thing I needed to do.

★ ★ ★

I was led up some stairs. An unpainted pine door. It was opened by a nurse — a middle-aged woman with Mongolian features. Inside, in a small room, Anichkova was reading to Yudin from a book with a red paper cover. I smiled, and indicated to her that she should continue. She read very slowly — it seemed to be some sort of children's story — occasionally stopping to ask him if he understood. She was very patient with him, very sweet. Eventually she shut the book, and said, 'Are you tired, Tolya?' He did not say anything. He did not seem to understand the question. Anichkova smiled at the nurse, who stepped forward and pulled him to his feet. Then, for the first time, he saw me. 'Hello, Anatoly Lvovich,' I said. Nothing — only the same stupid frightened smile. 'He doesn't know who I am,' I said.

'No.'

I took his hand and squeezed it, and patted him on the shoulder. When he and the nurse had left, I said to Anichkova, 'I want to ask you a few questions about him.'

'Okay.'

I knew a little about Anichkova. She had been
a Komsomol member — a very steady, sensible
young woman, from a Communist, working-
class family. She was married. Her husband,
whom she had met at the Urals State Technical
University, was also on the hospital staff. It
was while at the Urals State Technical
University that she had started informing for
the NKVD.

'You spend a lot of time with him, don't
you?' I said.

'Yes, I suppose so.'

'What does he do? How does he spend his
time?'

'How does he spend his time?' She frowned
thoughtfully. 'It's a bit of a strange question to
ask about someone like Tolya. It's such a
struggle for him to do the ordinary, everyday
things that he doesn't have much energy left
for anything else. We work with him, of course.'

'What do you mean you work with him? You
try to teach him?'

'We try to teach him, and we try to learn
from him as well. Which is the same thing,
really.'

I smiled. 'You've no reason, I suppose, to be
suspicious of him in any way?'

'No,' she said.

'I'll tell you why I ask.' And I told her about the warrant for his arrest that had been issued in 1942. 'He was a Nazi sympathiser,' I explained. 'He was also a famous pianist. Did you know that?' She said she did not. 'For years we thought he was dead, that he had been killed in the war. That's why it's taken so long to track him down. You're not surprised?'

'I'm surprised. I suppose.'

'So there's nothing you've noticed,' I said. 'Nothing suspicious?' She shook her head. 'I don't want to jeopardise your professional integrity in any way.'

'I know you don't.'

'Nothing questionable, strange, nothing at all?'

Smoking, she waited a while before shaking her head and saying, 'No, I don't think so.'

'Okay.' I stood up, and took my hat, and was about to thank her, when she said, 'Well, there is one thing.' She had obviously been wondering whether to say it.

'What?' I said.

'It's not necessarily suspicious.'

'What is it?'

'I mean . . . It's a bit strange.'

'What is?'

'His writing.'

'Whose?'

'Tolya's,' she said. 'Yudin's.'

When I told Lozovsky that I knew about Yudin's writing his face showed nothing, or only the slightest tightening of the jaw. 'Yes?' he said. I said I was surprised he hadn't mentioned it. 'Doctor Anichkova told you about it?' he said. 'It's not as significant as you probably think.'

'It seems significant.'

'It isn't. When you read what he's written, you'll see.' From one of his desk drawers — we were in his office — he took some exercise books, the sort that are used in schools. 'There,' he said. 'It's true that to a very limited extent he can read and write . . . You probably think it means he's less mentally impaired than you thought he was. It doesn't.' He lit a papirosa. 'When I first knew him he was obviously illiterate, and in any normal sense he still is. If he tries to write by thinking about what he's doing, he can't. It's hopeless. Just a mess. But if he doesn't think about it, if he just does it, without lifting the pencil from the paper, he can write quite well. It's another example of 'muscle memory', in fact. That is, it's his hand that still knows how to form the words, not his head. And in fact it's easier for him, in a way, to write than it is for him to speak. He can take his time. It's a very slow process. He puts sentences together very slowly, word by word. It takes him hours to write just a few words. The actual writing, putting the words down on paper, isn't the problem. The problem is finding the words in the first place. That's very difficult for him.'

I opened one of the exercise books. The unlined pages were filled with large, messy handwriting, and that each page had been written over several sessions was obvious from the variation in pencil quality, often from one line to the next. Turning them, I saw sentences, or parts of sentences:

The name of a teacher I had at school . . .
I imagine an enormous fly . . .
A lake surrounded by trees . . .

'If it's so difficult,' I said, 'why does he do it?'

Lozovsky said he did not know. Then he said, 'I suppose through writing he's able to make some sense, at least, of his existence. It also helps him piece together and understand the past. To some extent. He writes about the same few memories, mostly, over and over.'

'What memories?'

'Very early ones. That's normal in amnesia cases. I told you that.'

'What else does he write about?'

Lozovsky shrugged. 'His problems. He writes

about his problems in interacting with the world. Which I suppose is the only thing he has any first-hand knowledge of now.' He lit a papirosa with the end of the previous one. Then he said, 'The sad thing is, he seems to hope that through this writing he'll be able to find his way back to where he was when he was injured, and somehow pick up his life where he left off, and of course he won't.'

★   ★   ★

I know that Lozovsky had the highest esteem for Yudin. He once said to me, 'For him everything seems meaningless, and he still tries to make some sort of meaning out of it. He never succeeds, yet he still keeps trying to see his experience as something meaningful, to make some sort of meaning for himself. Misguidedly, you might say. I don't think so. That's what I'm doing in my work. That's what science is. And not just science.' Yudin was obviously a sort of inspiration for him. Perhaps that partly explains what happened later.

I still have one of the exercise books. The first one, written in 1945. The first entry takes up half a page — 'I've forgotten what whole things are like'. Underneath is scrawled, in smaller writing, 'no thoughts no memories'. And then, on the next page, 'I dont remember my

17

sisters names of my sisters'. The first few pages are like this. Then the entries start to get longer.

Because of my injury I've forgotten everything I ever learned or knew . . . I have to start again. Mostly it's because of my memory that I find it so hard to understand things. I've forgotten everything I ever knew. I have to learn like a child learns. I have the memory a child has . . .

The name of a teacher I had at school. Mariya Gavrilovna Lapshina. The names of my friends Sanka Mironov and Adya Protopopova and Volodka and Marusya.

Sometimes I remember who Lenin is. I remember I have a mother and sisters. Images like visions suddenly appear but I don't understand what they are . . .

Some vague thoughts suddenly come into my mind . . . I don't understand them. I try but I can't. They vanish. I can't remember them . . . Images of objects come into my mind. They vanish before I can understand what they are. Sometimes I remember words but they don't have any meaning . . .

Sometimes I remember who Lenin is. I remember I have a mother and sisters . . . Images like visions suddenly appear but I don't understand what they are . . . Since I was wounded I seem to be a newborn thing that just looks and listens but has no mind of its own . . .

I can remember my childhood even primary school. I remember the teacher I had at school Mariya Gavrilovna Lapshina and the names of my friends Sanka Mironov and Volodka Salomatin and Adya and Marusya. I go to Young Pioneers camp. I remember the camp and the things we did. I remember Sverdlovsk and parts of it and the whole town. Also my best friends Sanka Mironov and Volodka Salomatin and Adya Protopopova and Marusya Luchnikova. A teacher called Mariya Gavrilovna Lapshina.

I have hallucinations . . . I see something ugly. A human face with enormous ears . . . When I close my eyes I see millions of tiny insects. Or I see faces that frighten me. There's something strange and horrible about them. I can't see whole things. I know that sounds strange. I've forgotten what they look like . . .

Sometimes it seems like my head is enormous. That it's as big as a table ... Sometimes it seems like my head is very small like a coin. Sometimes I think my leg is near my shoulder. Above my head even. I know this can't be true but I still think that.

For some reason I can't remember anything. My head is completely empty and flat. No thoughts no memories ...

When a doctor asks me to show him where my nose is I can't do it. It's strange but I can't do it. I know the word nose is part of my body but I can't remember which part ... Because of my injury I can't remember which part it is. I've also forgotten the words for the parts of my body ...

A beautiful view everywhere. On one side a lake surrounded by pine trees. Wherever I look there are huge trees and the sky seems bluer even though the sun is shining just shining with light every-where ...

I see images of my childhood. The shore of the Iset where we used to swim ... The buildings where I went to kindergarten and primary school ... The faces of children and teachers I once knew. The strange thing is my memories are mostly from my childhood and primary school years. Those are the memories I live with now ...

I've seen dogs. I know what they look like but since my injury I haven't been able to imagine one. I can't imagine or draw a fly or a cat. I just can't imagine what they look like ... What I see are some specks or tiny bodies. I can't understand how wood is manufactured. What it's made of ...

I want to write about my life. What my life is like ... When I start I realise it's impossible because I can't remember the words I need. I spend so much time trying to remember the words I need ... In the end I stop trying because it hurts my head and makes me angry and upset ...

I've started to rewrite the whole thing but my mind seems to work more slowly. I don't seem to have the strength or memory. I have no thoughts or memories ... Most of the time I'm in a fog like a heavy half-sleep.

I wanted so much to write about my life and I worked so hard at it I finally felt sick. But this writing is my only way of thinking . . . If I stop I'll be back in that know-nothing world of emptiness and amnesia . . .

Is an elephant bigger than a fly? When I try to think about that I don't understand. I imagine an enormous fly. I don't understand what the question means. I know that sounds strange . . . What does bigger refer to? It can't be the fly. I understand that an elephant is big and a fly is small . . . I can't understand the question.

I stand in the middle of the room and try to exercise. I used to know different exercises I learned at Young Pioneers camp. I've forgotten them all. I just try various kinds of movements like raising and lowering my arms and sitting down and standing up. I don't enjoy these exercises. I get tired quickly and lose interest in exercising.

Memories suddenly appear. I see things like the river where we used to go swimming. The house where we lived. If I try to imagine these things at other times I can't do it. I can't picture them ... Sometimes I also remember people. Usually I can't remember them. Children and teachers I used to know ... Sanka Mironov and Volodka Salomatin and Adya Protopopova and ... There was a teacher ... We lived near a park where it was always very quiet ...

3

Sunday. Still no end to the heatwave. He has opened the windows, and the thin brown curtains, half-drawn to hold out the white intensity of the sun, move and swish in the warm draught. The sun sparkles through their loose mesh. It is late afternoon. Somewhere children are shouting, and the radio is on in Mrs Chakovsky's flat. There is, though, an atmosphere of stillness. The heat holds everything still. Sitting on the sofa in his underpants, he is reading the newspaper, though he knows it will just upset him — in Chile, Allende has formed a new government, and yet there is not a word, not a single word, about the way in which Kissinger is doing everything in his power to stymie his struggle for a socialist society there. Not a single word!

From the street, he hears the unfamiliar sound of a vehicle engine. With a short mechanical sigh — perhaps a well-timed stall — it stops. Holding open the curtain he sees Ivan emerging from his Lada. He seems to spot something, some imperfection, on its paintwork and scrubs it intently with the brown sleeve of his suit jacket. Then he makes

24

a minute adjustment to the wing mirror. Then, looking up and down the quiet suburban street, he locks the Lada, smoothes his moustache, and walks up the short concrete path under the cherry tree.

'You're late,' Aleksandr says, leading him up the stairs.

'There was a problem at work.'

'What problem?'

'Just . . . They want us to rewrite an article that was supposed to go to press today,' Ivan says. He is deputy editor of the main *oblast* newspaper, the *Urals Worker*.

Sitting on Aleksandr's mustard sofa — spartan in its square angles and lack of padding — he enthuses about his holiday in Yugoslavia. Not too much though. He knows Aleksandr's views on these things — on foreign travel, to Titoist Yugoslavia in particular — and does not want to upset him. Aleksandr has never left the Soviet Union, and says he never wants to. 'Why would I?' he says. Ivan does not know whether or not this is sincere. If it is, he does not understand it. He himself has travelled widely — to several of the fraternal nations of Eastern Europe. Even — one of the highlights of his entire life — to Tokyo, as a sports journalist for the 1964 Olympics.

Waiting for Aleksandr to dress, his eyes

move impassively from the spines of the books — so many books! — to the small postcard portrait of Stalin, smiling warmly in his white generalissimo's uniform. Involuntarily, Ivan wrinkles his nose and looks elsewhere. There are no images of the present leadership in the flat, of course. Nor even of Lenin. (In his office, Ivan has a modest alabaster head of Lenin, and there is an official photographic portrait of Brezhnev on the wall. These are not his own, though. They are part of the office furniture. In his flat there is a painting of Lenin in the hall, but that too is only for show.) Without thinking, he takes the pack of Golden Fleece from his pocket and lights one. There is, he notices, paper in the typewriter on Aleksandr's desk. He has been typing something. And next to the door a small square of whiter wall, where something used to hang. *What used to hang there?* he wonders. He should have an image of it in his mind. He is perspiring and wipes his face with a folded handkerchief.

The interior of the Lada is spotless, and the engine starts second time. However, it stalls as it moves out into the road, and Ivan has to restart it, which irritates him. He swears quietly, and sitting in the passenger seat, Aleksandr smiles to himself. 'How're the children?' he says, as they trundle slowly over

26

the untarmacked surface of the street. Ivan looks worried about his suspension. 'Um, I spoke to Shurik yesterday,' he says eventually. 'On the phone. He's got a German girlfriend.' Shurik, his younger son, is doing a postgraduate degree in Leipzig.

Scudding down Komsomol Street, with soot-black exhaust fumes in their wake, they overtake slow trams. The sun flares on the polished bonnet, and Ivan leans forward, squinting. They travel in tense silence — kick-off is in less than an hour now. It is only two weeks since the USSR finally and formally acknowledged the existence of West Germany as a state, with a seat at the United Nations, and West Berlin as part of it — and now they meet in the final of the European Championship. There seems to be something more than sport at stake. Aleksandr stares out the window. Trams and dusty trees. The long brown façade of the Urals State Technical University.

Ivan lives in a flat not far from 1905 Square. Looking at him in the slow lift — he himself is staring impassively into one of its polished walnut panels — Aleksandr says, 'Do you dye your hair, Vanya?'

Ivan looks up and smiles — a worried, self-effacing smile which makes Aleksandr think of the twelve-year-old who left their village and joined him in Sverdlovsk in 1929. Now his handsome teeth are nicotine-stained, and he is a man in his fifties, something which Aleksandr often forgets. There is a weariness, a sadness in the smile that was not there in 1929. 'Is it that obvious?' he says.

'For Agata, I suppose.'

'Actually she says she prefers it if I don't, but I don't believe her.'

There are a dozen people in the large living room of the eighth-floor flat. Agata, of course, heavily made up, serving drinks. Andrey, Ivan's older son, and his pregnant wife. A man with a little white beard, wearing a beige cardigan — Spiridon, one of Ivan's subordinates on the paper. He hovers nervously, not saying much. Some other friends of Ivan's — men and women in smart clothes, smelling of scent — whom Aleksandr does not know. It is unusual for him to be included in these sorts of events.

In startlingly lifelike colour (some people ooh and ah — Ivan looks momentarily pleased) the teams file out onto the green pitch — the West Germans in white, the Soviets in red — and the national anthems are played. Khurtsilava and Beckenbauer shake hands in the centre circle. The teams take up their positions. In the warm living room Aleksandr is shivering slightly. It seems to him that he has never wanted anything as much as he wants the Soviet Union to win this match. The Austrian referee blows his whistle. It starts.

The tension immediately takes on a new quality. Smooth, sickening, panicky. For the first few minutes every touch seems loaded with terrifying significance. Every incipient attack is met with shouts of joy and aggression if it is the red shirts surging forward, fumbling terror if it is the Germans. After a while, however, a sort of enervated lethargy sets in. Aleksandr finds himself oddly uninterested in the minutiae of the match, the indecisive midfield play. For a moment, he even looks away from the screen — through the blue fug of cigarette smoke everyone's eyes are on the television set. Even the women, standing in the low arch through to the shadowy hall. It is quiet, except for the measured, nervous voice of the commentator, and the occasional scrape of someone lighting a cigarette. Then Müller scores. From the television, there is a long explosion of white noise. It is the only sound in the smoke-filled living room. Everyone is staring at the screen in shock. The ball is in the net. White-shirted Germans are sprinting, smiling, sprawling on the turf. It's as though someone's died.

Within moments of the second half starting

— some people have not even retaken their seats — they score a second. This time, as Wimmer is mobbed by his ecstatic team-mates, the ensuing silence lasts much longer — is in fact still more or less in place when, six minutes later, Müller surges through, and with an extraordinary shot extinguishes whatever unspoken hope still lingered in the sweltering living room. They watch what is left with silent loathing. Kick-off seems a long time ago, seems to have taken place in another world. It was another world — a world of wonderful possibility, that is now a world of sour outcome. The Soviet players are struggling to hold the strutting Germans. They have stopped tackling. They look shocked. The three shrill notes of the final whistle sound, and the winners — shaggy as hippies, skinny as drug addicts — fling their fists in the air. Rudakov sits slouched in front of his goal. Khurtsilava has tears in his eyes. When the King of Belgium hands Becken-bauer the silver trophy, Ivan turns off the television. The last image they see on the fading screen is Beckenbauer hoisting the trophy over his head. He is not even smiling.

Outside, night has fallen on Sverdlovsk. Some people leave immediately, as if the loss existed only there, in Ivan's flat. The others, understanding that it is not so easily escaped, turn to drink. Within an hour of the final whistle, Agata — who has made a smudgy mess of her lipstick — is insisting in a loud voice that Michelangelo's David is a portrait of Leonardo da Vinci, while Spiridon opens a bottle of pepper vodka with a single very small — and therefore all the more sinister-looking — chilli suspended in it. He pours himself a huge measure and slugs it down. Immediately his high pink forehead twinkles with perspiration, which forms fat drops on the tip of his nose and in his white moustache. A minute earlier he had been shouting that Leonardo da Vinci was dead — *dead!* — when Michelangelo made the David. Now he sits there silently staring into space with a sullen look in his eyes. 'Spiridon!' shouts one of Ivan's friends, a large man in a loud suit, pouring more shots. 'Spiridon!' Spiridon looks at him mournfully. 'Spiridon! To the team! They did their best! To the team . . . ' Someone stands up and hits their skull on the low overhead light. The shadows sway wildly, as they would on a ship at sea. There is the sound of something smashing.

It is past midnight when Ivan drives Aleksandr home. Drunk, he steers slowly through the quiet streets. Aleksandr is untalkative. 'You okay?' Ivan says.

'I'm just thinking about something.'

'The football?'

Aleksandr shakes his head. Then, a moment later, he murmurs, 'Metelyev Log.'

'What?'

'Metelyev Log.'

'What's that?' Ivan takes a hand off the plasticated wheel to fish his cigarettes from his pocket and the Lada wanders in the road. 'There was a strike or something,' he says. 'A railway strike. Was that it?'

'No, that wasn't it.'

They have left the tarmacked streets and are probing the mothy darkness of suburban tracks.

'There was a man called Lozovsky,' Aleksandr says. 'He was a sort of doctor.'

'Was he?'

'Yes. You wrote a piece on him.'

'Did I?'

'Two, in fact.'

Leaning forward with a cigarette in his mouth, peering through the windscreen, the speckle of impacted insects, Ivan says, 'Do you know how many thousands of pieces I've written?'

'You've forgotten?'

There is a long silence. Then Ivan says, 'Sasha, what's the point of talking about these

32

things? Nobody wants to hear about them now . . . '

'*You* don't . . . '

'No, I don't. I'm surprised *you* do . . . '

'Surprised? Why are you surprised?'

Ivan sighs. 'I don't know. Forget it. We're here.'

4

Ivan, you sometimes seem to have no memory at all. So let me tell you: You were not always like you are now. Once you were known for finding stories that made your superiors nervous. The story of the 'strike', for instance. You mentioned it last night. The story of the 'strike'. I took you out to lunch — in those days I took you to lunch — and you told me about it.

It was just after my first visit to Metelyev Log. I was stranded there for more than a week. A mudslide somewhere in the hills had stopped the trains. When I finally got home, Irishka said you were looking for me. I went to see you on Sunday. You weren't in. Katya opened the door. She was heavily pregnant with Shurik. Whenever I saw her, she talked and talked about you — how she was worried about you, how you were not eating enough, how you worked too hard, smoked too much, didn't sleep properly. She spent her life worrying about you, Ivan. I asked her where you were, and she said you were working — on Sunday, she said, you had to write the paper for Monday. This wasn't true, and she must have known it. You wrote Monday's paper on Friday.

I took you out to lunch the next day. You were late, of course. You were wearing a jacket that was several sizes too big for you and an open-necked shirt with long collars. Your hair, parted in the middle, was plastered shinily to your head. You were smoking a Belomor. That was how you looked in those days. We ordered our lunch, and then I said, 'So there's something you want to tell me about?'

'Yes,' you said, 'something I'm working on.' That was what I had expected. In those days you often told me what you were working on. You took a piece of paper out of your pocket. 'This,' you said.

'What is it?'

'It's a letter,' you said, unhurriedly, salting your bread, 'from the management committee of the Molotov railway to the oblispolkom, here in Sverdlovsk.' It will probably surprise you to know that I still have it. The very letter. It says:

At present we are unable to pay any wages, as has been the case for several weeks. Workers cannot buy even a single kilogram of bread, and are coming to work hungry and declaring that they do not have the strength to work. Having been deprived of bread and food products, the dependants and children of workers are forced to starve, and the workers themselves are dividing up what little we can give them with their children and thereby driving themselves to emaciation. This failure to pay wages is now acquiring a political character. Non-appearance for work is becoming more widespread, and there have been instances of engine drivers refusing to take their locomotives out. For all these reasons, and in view of the vital strategic importance of the railway, we urge the immediate release of the emergency funds necessary to resolve this exceptionally difficult situation.

In the Ural restaurant, tucking into the zakouski — some smoked trout, some pickled garlic, some cucumber and sour cream — you said, 'Do you think the necessary funds were released?'
'I've no idea.'
With a flourish, you produced a second letter, obviously an answer to the first, written several days later, from the office of the oblispolkom secretary for transport.

The government's decree (15 February 1948) forbids the covering of losses of economic organisations. Thus the railway and its economic units are obliged to take all measures not only to make good the circulating capital which they allowed to be exhausted in 1947, but to find additional sources of accumulation, and to achieve the stable financial position of their subdivisions.

'Where did you get these letters?' I said.

'They were sent to me anonymously at the paper.'

'It's probably embezzlement.'

'Possibly.'

I made a little speech. I said, 'The state can't keep pouring money into the pockets of managers who steal from their enterprises. Something has to be done about it. It amounts to sabotage. And the ordinary workers are the ones who suffer. It's good that you're writing about it. We need to increase people's awareness of this. These people need to be exposed and dealt with. It's the only long-term solution — '

'It may be a case of embezzlement,' you said, interrupting me, 'or it may not. That isn't the point.'

'Oh, isn't it? What is the point?'

'The point is what happened next.'

'Which was?'

'There was a strike.'

'What do you mean?'

'What do you think?' You were almost whispering, leaning towards me over your now empty plate with a newly lit papirosa in your hand. 'There was an organised, coordinated strike, which lasted for several days.'

Suddenly you sat back and smiled. The waitress — the pretty one you liked so much — put our lunch on the table.

'A strike?' I said, when she had moved away. You nodded, holding your spoon. 'What makes you think that?'

'I have several sources,' you said. 'And there have been massive disruptions on the railway.'

'Not necessarily caused by a strike. The disruptions could have been caused by something else.'

'Like what?'

'I don't know. A mudslide, for instance.'

Stirring your soup, you smiled knowingly. 'A mudslide?'

'For instance,' I said.

'Well, as it happens, that's exactly what they're saying.'

'Who?'

'The management of the railway, and the oblispolkom. They're saying there was a mudslide, but they're very vague about where. Very vague indeed.'

'What are you saying?'

'I don't think there was a mudslide.' You started to eat.

'Why?'

'Sasha,' you said with your mouth full, 'one mudslide wouldn't shut the whole railway!'

'It depends where it was.'

'The strike started with the engine drivers,' you said, 'and spread very quickly. The whole workforce was refusing to work until they were paid — '

'You're not planning to write about this?' I said suddenly.

'Why not? You said it would be good to write about it.'

'Don't be stupid! You know what I meant. It would be good for you to write about the embezzlement that led to the situation described in those letters. The strike, if there was one, isn't the point. It's nothing to do with the underlying problems. You mustn't write about it.' In those days I worried about you, Ivan. Your name was mentioned in the wrong places. It was starting to appear on the wrong lists. I know you wanted to be successful. You wanted to be editor of 'Pravda'. What you did not seem to understand was that nothing could be worse for your prospects of success than the sort of name you were making for yourself. I don't know why you didn't understand that.

Perhaps because you had started your journalistic career with such a shocking, sensational exposé — the fact that the sons and daughters of obkom members were being awarded degrees from the Urals State Technical University, including medical degrees, without having passed the exams. Publicly you were feted for that. Unfortunately, it also made you enemies. I know it frustrated you to see your more politically skilful peers move into positions of editorial power, or to Moscow to work on the nationals, while you were still sent out to Uralmash to interview Stakhanovites. I know you were desperate to make some sort of mark, something that would be reprinted — as the Urals State exposé was — in the national press. You may have thought the strike story would do that. It wouldn't. And there was no shortage of people willing to stab you in the back if you made such a stupid mistake. I don't know if you ever understood quite what a precarious position you were in. I understood, and I was worried about you. I knew you saw me as a sort of protection. There was, though, a limit to what I would be able to do, which was why I said, 'You must not write about it.'

Later, we walked along Lenin Prospekt. You were sullen. 'Listen,' I said, 'I understand the suffering of those workers, but a strike — if there was one — would be seen as a hostile political act. To publicise it wouldn't help them. Not that it would be published, if you wrote about it. And writing about it wouldn't help you either. Quite the opposite. So what would be the point? You've got to forget about it, the whole thing.'

Sulkily, smoking, you watched a tram pass. It was early spring, everything was wet. I see the exact moment, the sodden wooden pavement, the expression on your face. I thought I understood you then. I thought we were essentially the same. We were both saved from village life by Yevdokimov, who made it possible for us — first me, then you — to go to school in Sverdlovsk. He understood the urgent need to establish a working-class intelligentsia, which unlike the old tsarist specialists on whom we were still dependent in those years, would be progressive in its instincts. When we arrived in Sverdlovsk, we were not aware — were we? — that our education was part of an effort to do this. What is undeniably true is that it would have been impossible for us to have had such an education before 1917. Our lives would have been like those of our parents — illiterate, ignorant, impoverished, without hope. That they were not, the opportunities that we have had, we owe entirely to the party.

'Who were your sources for this?' I said. 'How can you trust them? You pay them, I suppose?

Slip them a bottle of vodka?'

'I trust them.'

'Perhaps you should let me have those letters.'

'Why?'

'I'll look into it. There may be something . . . ' I shrugged. Without enthusiasm you handed me the letters — I did not want them to be found in your possession, that was why I took them from you. 'Have you mentioned this to anyone else?' I said.

'Of course not.'

'Not to Katya?'

'No.'

'And not to . . . You know who I mean.'

You paused, perhaps stung by this — were you stung by it? — and then shook your head.

★ ★ ★

That spring was the time of the Zhdanovshchina. Another word you will have forgotten, Ivan. You knew it once. The Zhdanovshchina. People's minds are formed by what they see and hear — a lifetime in journalism has surely taught you that — and if, for instance, Leningrad's literary journals were obsessed with the most nihilistic modern writing from the West, it undermined our efforts to move towards Communism, to move towards it in

42

people's minds. That was the most important thing. I therefore spent much of my time interviewing members of the intelligentsia about their work. Unfortunately, some of the others took a very negative approach to this, laughing at poems in front of the people who had written them, and saying, 'Who would want to read this? What does this have to do with the everyday lives of ordinary people?' Or looking exaggeratedly pained as someone's music was played, and then shouting, 'Why would anyone want to listen to that? The average person wants music they can hum!' Such philistinism succeeded only in turning people against us.

My experience of this sort of work was probably why I was sent to interview Yudin in the first place. To prepare myself, I made a summary of his security file. There were a number of photographs in the file, mostly of Yudin himself. He was shortish, stocky and muscular, with dark brown hair and blue eyes. One photograph, taken from the end-of-year album of the Moscow Conservatory, 1939, shows a thoughtful-looking young man, turning his face slightly from the camera, the hint of a half-ironic smile on his lips. A sensitive face, though not a delicate one — the eyebrows emphatic, the nose prominent. Unfortunately, the evidence against this thoughtful-looking young man was strong.

His professor at the Conservatory was Heinrich Haussman, a German married to a Russian woman. He seems to have been a father-figure to Yudin. Often, outside school hours, Yudin would spend time with Haussman and his family. He would spend weekends at the dacha. His enthusiasm for bourgeois German culture, however, seems to have pre-dated his friendship with Haussman. He learnt German at school and spoke it well by the time he arrived in Moscow in 1936. He read German books, and specialised as a performer in the works of J.S. Bach. The file said that 'he often compares Russian composers unfavourably with German ones, especially Bach'. (And next to the name 'Bach' some oaf had written 'Fascist? Nazi? FIND OUT'.) He wrote an essay called 'The Meaning of Form and the Form of Meaning in the Music of J.S. Bach', which was published in the leading Soviet musical journal in December 1938.

In February 1939 he won first prize in the Tchaikovsky International piano competition. In March he moved into a new flat on Kutuzov Prospekt. In June he went to the Crimea, where he had use of a villa overlooking the sea. He was in the Crimea for most of the summer. Photos from his time there: horsing around by the pool, posing, eating dinner at a long table in the open air, everyone looking tanned and healthy, even the Azerbaijani housemaids. His mother and sisters came to visit. Haussman spent a week there. There was a photo — sad in view of what was to happen — of Yudin, smiling hugely (he had very straight white teeth), with one arm around Haussman and the other around his mother.

In September, he started his recording of the forty-eight preludes and fugues of Bach's 'Well-tempered Clavier'. This piece had been recorded only once before, by the Swiss Edwin Fischer in 1936. It was considered desirable that the Soviet Union equal this feat. There was also the prospect of an international market for recordings by Yudin. The final session was on April 6 1940. The following spring, however, the recording was withdrawn. This was done for political reasons — by then the leadership was preparing the country psychologically for a war with Germany, and German music was no longer politically correct. Yudin protested, of course. He appealed to Haussman for help, but Haussman was himself German — and was deported that spring, accused of Fascism and spying, and died during the war in unknown circumstances. This deprived Yudin of his mentor and father-figure — his own father had died years earlier — at a time when his world seemed suddenly to be falling apart. In particular, newspaper articles were appearing denouncing his devotion to German music. German, Germany, Germans, words that in the winter of 1940–41 start to appear more and more frequently in the file. He had been to Germany. He knew and corresponded with several German nationals. On at least one occasion he had expressed admiration for the Hitlerite regime.

He entered the army in the late summer of 1941. However, in June, just after the invasion, he had attempted to contact Haussman, sending the letter via a Swiss musician, Albert Zugzwang in Luzern. In this letter he spoke of his desire to leave the USSR, and go to Germany 'where I have so many friends'. It was intercepted. In any case, Haussman may already have been dead. Then, in April 1942 Yudin wrote, again via Zugzwang, to Rudolf Steglich, a friend of his, a German musicologist and a member of the Nazi party. Like the first letter, this one, which was also intercepted, inquired whether it would be possible for him to go to Germany. In it he speaks of his belief in the superiority of German culture, and of his love for the country. He even seems to imply that he would welcome a German victory in the war. In view of this, it was decided to take action, and on May 17 a warrant was issued for his arrest, something not mentioned in the obituaries published several weeks later. Such were the known facts when I went to see him at Metelyev Log in April 1948.

★   ★   ★

Then, one evening in May, I was summoned to Mikhalkov's office on the fourth floor of the old MGB building.

Mikhalkov was in with someone so I had to wait for a few minutes, making small talk with his secretary, old Yegorova, who had worked there for a succession of colonels since the twenties. Some civilians in suits emerged from the inner office and left hurriedly. 'You can go in now,' Yegorova said. Mikhalkov was sitting at his desk. Sherepin was there too. 'They want to have a look at Yudin,' Mikhalkov said, without preamble. 'I know it's not what you suggested.'

'No.'

'You think it's unnecessary to move him from where he is?'

I said nothing.

'They just want to have a look at him,' Mikhalkov said. 'They want a second medical opinion. That's what I think. They don't entirely trust this Lozovsky. One of our long-nosed friends, I presume?'

'One of our . . . ?'

'A Jew.'

47

'Oh. Yes, I think so.'

Sherepin nodded slowly several times, staring at the floor as though his mind was on something else.

'What do you make of him?' Mikhalkov said to me.

'Lozovsky?'

'Yes.'

I said I knew him slightly, having spent a week staying with him and his wife, and saw no reason not to trust him. I did not mention his initial failure to tell me about Yudin's writing. I myself had wondered whether to mention it in my submission. I had to, of course, and I suspect that it was this, more than anything else, that weighed against him.

5

On the radio they are talking about the first test flight of the new Soyuz spacecraft. It was entirely successful, they say. There is a momentary pause, then the next news item. '*Prime Minister Major Fidel Castro in a message to the people and leaders of the Soviet Union, which was sent from the aeroplane in which he returned to Cuba following his visit to the USSR, states that . . .*'

He slides one of the old suitcases out from under his bed. The one full of papers — old letters and documents, small photographs, forgotten literary efforts. He is searching for his chess set, and even the minimal exertion of his searching is making him sweat. Like everyone else, he has a sudden interest in the game. Eventually he finds it. The small wooden pieces are wrapped in a sheet of newspaper, and he sees from the text that he has not played since the Caribbean Crisis of 1962. The board is a folding piece of card — or was, until the fold wore out and it fell apart.

In the living room, the radio is still

reporting Castro's message. ' . . . emphasises that the friendship of the two nations has been forged in the thirteen years since the victory of the Cuban Revolution, and is based on the common struggle against US imperialism. The message also refers to the feats of the Soviet people in the political economic, social scientific-technical and military fields, which are unprecedented in history . . . ' He turns the frequency knob until he finds a voice from Reykjavik. Then he lines up the two halves of the board, and puts out the pieces.

There is a little click, as Boris Vasilyevich, playing white, makes the first move of the match. The commentator says, 'Spassky, pawn to d4.' Aleksandr moves the white king pawn forward two squares. The radio is silent, except for the occasional soft cough from the audience. Fischer, as has been explained, is not there. Nobody knows where he is.

His photo is on the front of this week's *Soviet Sport*. Aleksandr holds the paper up and inspects it — the huge face with its little sunken eyes. There is something insane about them. Fischer looks like he hasn't slept in days. His hair is a mess; his mouth hangs slightly open. There is also a photo of Boris Vasilyevich. Next to Fischer he exudes a sincere, serious dignity. Aleksandr looks at his watch — two minutes have passed since he played pawn d4. Quietly, the commentator interrupts the silence to say, 'Fischer has still not arrived. I remind you that if he has not arrived within one hour, he will forfeit the game.'

Minutes pass, and he looks over the profile of Fischer in *Soviet Sport*. *Fischer's social and political development are as stunted as his emotional development. He is not married and has no friends. A member of a profiteering Christian fundamentalist sect, he loathes everything politically progressive. His ambition is to get rich, and money is his principal motivation. He agreed to take part in the World Championship match in Reykjavik only when a British millionaire doubled the prize fund to $250,000 . . . His contempt for women is well documented. In an interview he states: 'They're all weak, all women. They're stupid compared to men.' More disturbing still is his anti-Semitism. 'There are too many Jews in chess,' he insists. 'They seem to have taken away the class of the game. They don't seem to dress so nicely, you know.' This despite the fact that his own mother is Jewish . . . At the chessboard he tries to intimidate his opponents with his overbearing personality, and will storm out like a spoilt child if playing conditions are not* to his exact liking. A spoilt child, of course, is exactly what Fischer is. This, some might say, is the inevitable fate of the child prodigy, but let us not forget that Spassky too was a prodigy, winning the Soviet championship at seventeen. Learning his chess in Leningrad after the war, this son of a peasant mother and labourer father has found a rather more sober maturity: while Fischer, at the age of twenty-nine, reads nothing but puerile comics with names like Spiderman and Batman, Spassky reads Dostoyevsky. While Fischer indulges in fantasies about living in a house shaped like a rook, Spassky works hard to raise a family . . .

Next to the profile is another, smaller photo of Fischer in which he is being fitted with a suit, a tailor in the background, chalking marks on the half-made, one-sleeved jacket. Fischer's hands are on his hips and he is looking at the camera with a joyless smile on his big face, a smile that expresses nothing but self-regard and contempt for the world. Here, Aleksandr thinks, is a man who has not engaged with the world except through chess and money. He has not engaged with the world morally in any way . . .

Suddenly, the radio registers a whispering commotion, the unsettling of an audience. 'He's here,' the commentator says grimly.

'He's arrived. Fischer has arrived. Seven minutes late. He's coming onto the stage. Spassky stands. They shake hands. Fischer takes his seat. What is . . . Oh he's played. He's played knight f4.'

Aleksandr moves the black knight out to f4, and stares thoughtfully at the board.

It is Spassky's move.

'Pawn c4,' announces the commentator.

★　★　★

Hours later, and the living room is full of hot evening sunlight. The windows are open, and outside children are playing in the street — he hears their loud shouts. The board on the desk has developed into a fixed, complex position. It is evenly balanced — both players have a bishop and six pawns. It is a drawn position. The radio fizzes tensely. 'Pawn b4 to b5.' The commentator's voice is tense, and tired. Aleksandr advances the white pawn, and waits for Fischer's move. 'Bishop d6 takes h2. That's a blunder,' says the commentator. There is a quiet murmur in the hall. Aleksandr makes the move. He doesn't see . . .

'Pawn g2 to g3.'

The commentator sounds less tired.

Oh, yes. The bishop's snared. Aleksandr

frowns, displeased that he did not see it. 'The game has been transformed,' whispers the commentator excitedly. 'It's been transformed. It seemed like it was heading for a certain draw. Spassky was playing for the draw, exchanging at every opportunity. Fischer wasn't satisfied with the draw. But he was too aggressive. An extraordinary blunder. Now, surely, he's going to lose.'

As night falls on Sverdlovsk, the endgame drags on — the patient, slow-motion game of kings and pawns. Fischer is struggling to survive with pawns against pawns and bishop. Spassky is struggling to finish him off. In the end, when moths are bumping almost silently into the light bulb that hangs from the ceiling, the game is adjourned until tomorrow. Applause — he switches off the radio, stopping it short, and stares at the position of the pieces. Silent little pieces of wood whose significant positions are tonight transfixing the world.

★　★　★

He wakes very early in the morning. Even this early the air is soupily warm. There is a very fine mist in the street. He sits down at his desk, and suddenly the strokes of the typewriter smash the early morning peace.

Spring
had
transformed
the
forest

He stops. He is about to tell the story of how he went to Metelyev Log for the second time, when spring had transformed the forest. However, there is something that he omitted from the story of his first visit. Then, for most of the time, it rained. His memories of the place are mostly of rainy weather — of misty rain that glistened on the nap of coarse cloth, like the grey collar of her coat.

There was only one sunny day while he was there — he woke to find the knotholes in the window shutters fiercely white. From somewhere outside he heard the slow strokes of an axe. The sun was warm. Insects sported in its warmth. The sound of the axe was coming from the side of the house, where the wood pile was, and there, on a scarred tree stump, she was splitting logs into smaller pieces. Later, they went for a walk. Unselectively, the sun highlighted small pieces of the forest. He was not dressed for the sort of walk she had in mind, in his suit trousers and waistcoat and filthy shirt. His leather-soled shoes slipped on the wet clay, and he walked more slowly than she did, stopping to peer into the long shadowy perspectives of the wood, where the light shape-shifted under the trees when the wind, softly, moved their foliage.

'I saw a bear once,' she said.

'Here?'

She nodded. 'It was just walking along. I don't think it saw me.'

'Were you scared?'

'No. Maybe I should have been.'

'Maybe. What time of year was it?'

'This time of year. Spring. Two years ago.'

'Then you should have been scared,' he said. 'It's this time of year they're most dangerous, when they've just come out of hibernation and they're starving.'

'I know. So I stood very still and watched it walk past. It was about . . . fifty metres away, moving through the trees. Slowly, not in a hurry. Sometimes it lifted its head and sniffed the wind. Then suddenly I had an impulse to make a noise, to shout out.'

'I hope you didn't.'

'I shouted, *'I'm here!'* ' He thought she was joking and laughed. Then she said, 'I did.' And when he still looked sceptical, as if he did not know whether to take her seriously or not, 'Yes, I did.'

'Why?'

'I don't know.'

'What did it do?'

'What do you think? It looked at me. I don't know if it saw me. Even then I wasn't scared. I just wondered if it would kill me. For a long time it didn't move. It seemed like a long time. It was probably only a few seconds. Then it walked on.'

'I see. Well please don't do that if we see one today.'

She laughed.

The forest had a strangely empty look. The narrow trunks of the pines were as straight as pencils, the only branches higher up, where there was sunlight. They were walking on fallen pine needles — epochs of them, as she pointed out — and it was like walking on a mattress.

He told her that he was originally from a village, and had lived there until he was twelve. 'I've forgotten almost everything about it now.'

'Forgotten what?'

'For instance, how to milk a cow. When I was a child I had to help my parents with the milking.'

She seemed uninterested, and lit a papirosa.

The path went straight up an ivy-covered slope. Initially, he mistook the sound of water for the wind. Only when the wind stopped, and the whole forest stood very still for a moment, did he understand that what he was hearing was water — an unvarying high soft sound. And then, quite suddenly, unmistakably watery. In the shifting shade under the trees, the stream flowed down a natural stairway of stones, shallow pools perpetually overflowing. The air was empty, pure. The shadows had the frigidity of early spring. From an open space they were able to turn and see the lake in its valley, and the monumental clouds mirrored in its surface, which was perfectly still. The soil was waterlogged, and soaked through the seat of his trousers.

They walked slowly down. It was mid-afternoon, warm and sleepy, when her house was visible through the trees at the end of its short path. He waited on the wooden steps for her to unlock the door. 'Oh I forgot to lock it,' she said. She opened it and went in. Immediately he heard Lozovsky's voice — 'Nadya? Have you seen the Chekist?' The impersonal tone of this hurt his feelings. He had been there, living with them, for more than a week. 'Oh, you're here,' Lozovsky said. It was quite dark inside the house. Lozovsky was smiling. 'Well, good news,' he said.

'What's that?'

'The line's open.'

'The line?'

'The railway line.'

'What, already?'

'We got a telegram an hour ago.' He lit the unlit papirosa that he was holding. 'The train will be through at the usual time today. You don't look very pleased,' he said, through the smoke.

'Of course I'm pleased.'

Sitting at his desk, staring at the typewriter, he is suddenly aware of the spectral thunder of a jet. A vapour trail is visible in the sky. The plane itself is not visible. Silently, in the stratosphere, the trail disperses. He spends very little time away from his flat. A fortnight in the Crimea every summer, a KGB sanatorium on the sea. Swimming in the hot sulphurous pools. Perhaps an excursion to the Nikitsky Botanical Gardens in Yalta. That's all. And even that seems too much — especially when he has to pack his small suitcase, and sit waiting for the loud honk of the bus when it stops in front of the house. Unhappy, silent, slightly lost, he takes his seat among the others, in their short-sleeved shirts and sunglasses, and slowly they wind through the eastern suburbs of the city. Then out to Koltsovo. He first flew in a plane the year Gagarin went to space. That flight, like all the others he has made since, was between

Sverdlovsk and Simferopol. In the years before that they would spend several days on the train, slowly leaving the stress of their work, which they never talked about, while the shadows of trees flickered on their sleeping faces. The vapour trail has dispersed. The sky's mineral blue is intact. He sits down at his desk and stares at the words he has typed.

6

Spring had transformed the forest. Nor was the hospital, an inelegant weather-stained neo-classical pile, quite like my memory of it. Since it had been demilitarised in 1947, we needed the director's permission if we wanted to take one of the patients. There was a form he needed to sign, known as a form four-eighty. This Lozovsky would not do. He would not sign it. Having vouched for him in Mikhalkov's office only forty-eight hours earlier, I found I took this personally. I sighed. I said, 'Mikhail Naumovich, I feel we know each other, if only slightly, and I want to be open with you.' He was obviously upset, though he tried not to show it. 'They want a second medical opinion,' I said. 'There are things that aren't easy to understand if you haven't met him. The writing in particular. You know that. It's why you didn't tell me about it yourself.' He said nothing and lit a papirosa. 'I understand why they want a second opinion,' I said. 'I hope you do as well.'

'Does it matter?'

'Does what matter?'

'Does it matter whether I understand?'

'I hope you do.'

'Then let's say I do.'

The next morning, when I went to his office for the form, he said he had not signed it yet, he wanted to look at it first. This seemed odd, since he must have seen many like it in the past. Nevertheless, I said, 'Of course,' and sat down on the old leather sofa. He spent a long time looking at the form. Finally he said, 'No, I can't sign this.'

'Why not?'

'Have you read it?'

'Yes.'

'So you must understand.'

'Understand what?'

'Well I think it's quite obvious . . . '

'Just sign it, please.'

For several seconds he said nothing. Then: 'No. It wants me to state that the patient is mentally and physically fit to be transported, and to face interrogation, and a trial. And he isn't.'

When he had said this, in a quiet voice, he stared at me. He was even smiling slightly. I think I knew then that he would never sign the form. I saw the stubbornness in his eyes. And what stubbornness! He was a man who in an earlier time would have died at the stake out of sheer stubbornness and vanity. Still, I tried to persuade him.

'They want a second opinion,' I said. 'A second medical opinion. You can understand that, surely?'

'Then let them send someone here.'

'No. They won't do that.'

When he just sat there, staring at me, I stood up and went to the window, wondering what to do. 'I'll make a note,' I said, 'of your objections to this. Your purely medical objections. I'll also allow Doctor Anichkova to accompany Yudin. To make sure he's okay. Strictly speaking it's not allowed . . .' Lozovsky said nothing. 'Okay?'

'That's not the point.'

'What isn't?'

'It doesn't matter whether Anichkova goes with him or not. What difference does that make?'

'Well you're worried about his welfare, aren't you?' I shouted. 'I assume that's what you're worried about.'

'Yes, it is . . .'

'And do you really think your not signing this form will help him?'

'I don't know,' he said. 'I know that signing it wouldn't.'

'You're wrong. What do you think will happen if you don't sign it?'

'I don't know . . .'

'Then I'll tell you! It won't make any

difference! Not for him.'

He did not like being shouted at.

'Look,' I said. 'I understand why you're opposed to this. I'll do everything possible to make sure he's okay. You have my word. It's just for a second opinion. So sign it. Please.' He did not move. There was a long silence. I said, 'I'm leaving later this afternoon. I hope — I do hope — you'll have signed it by then.'

He had not, which saddened me. Though many people would not have, I liked Lozovsky. The first time I was there, he and his wife were very kind to me. I was there for so long that I started to feel like part of the family. They made an effort to make me feel at home, and I helped in whatever ways were needed. I sawed logs for firewood, fetched water from the well. His wife was younger than he was. In fact, she had been one of his pupils at the Second Medical Institute in Moscow. They were handsome, intelligent people. We ate together in the evenings, and talked. There was usually an element of friendly sparring to these talks — with Lozovsky that was inevitable. Often he and I played chess. He was a strong player. We were evenly matched, I would say. Sometimes he played the piano. There was a piano in their little wooden house, an imported German upright, looking very out of place in the forest. He told me one evening how it had been transported there, on a horse-drawn wagon through knee-deep mud. He said he had wanted to be a professional musician. He wasn't talented enough. To me he seemed very talented. I have a memory, in particular, of his playing the A major prelude from the second book of the 'Well-tempered Clavier' — those preludes and fugues were what he usually played — a memory of an evening in the wet forest, and that sad, placid music.

★   ★   ★

From the station, I went straight to the office. It was late — a vacuum cleaner was whining somewhere — and I had to tell Mikhalkov what had happened.

However, he seemed no more than vaguely interested in what I had to say, which surprised me. 'Why didn't he sign it?' he said. 'I don't know.' He looked at his watch. 'It's almost ten,' he said. 'I shouldn't still be here.' He told Sherepin to phone for his car, and then, just as I was leaving, he said, 'Do you want a lift, Aleksandr Andreyevich?' It was the first time he had ever offered me a lift. 'If you want one,' he said, pulling on his overcoat, 'meet me at the front entrance in five minutes.' It was obvious that he wanted to speak to me in private, so I waited for him in the lobby and when he arrived we went out to where his Packard was waiting in a sudden downpour. I held the umbrella and opened the door for him and then hesitated, not knowing where to sit myself. Perhaps I was expected to sit in the front with the driver. Mikhalkov immediately moved over, however. 'There's been a slight change of plan,' he said. 'I'm going to see Veklishev at his flat.' General Veklishev was the head of the oblast MGB, and for an uneasy moment I thought he meant for me to join him. Then he said, 'Pyotr will drop me there, then take you on. Where do you live?'

I told him.

'Did you get that, Pyotr?'

Pyotr nodded.

'Yes,' Mikhalkov said, with a sigh. 'Veklishev wants to know what's going on. With Yudin. He's taking a personal interest in this one. And you know what he's like. When he gets hold of something.' Needless to say, I did not know what he was like. I had never spoken more than a few words to him.

'I'm sorry about this problem,' I said. 'With Lozovsky.'

Mikhalkov yawned. 'It's not your fault. Lozovsky will have to be moved. We need someone who'll sign the form. Who's his deputy?'

'A man called Dyomkin.'

66

'Do you know him?'

'I've met him.'

'Will he sign it?'

'Yes, probably.'

'Okay. It will have to be done through the oblispolkom, of course. We'll have to speak to them about it. That's our next move. The man to speak to is Gasselblat.'

'Gasselblat.'

'Yes. Explain the situation to him. Arrange to meet him — meet him personally, don't do it over the phone. Make him understand what needs to be done.'

We pulled over in front of a tall building. It stood out in the darkness because of the way that many of its windows were lit, even at that hour, with electric light. 'Here we are,' Mikhalkov said. 'Pyotr will take you on. Wait for me here when you've dropped him, Pyotr. I shouldn't be long.'

Pyotr turned the Packard in the wide road. 'How are you, Pyotr?' I shouted over the noise of the engine and the squeaking of the windscreen wiper.

For a moment, he half-turned. 'How d'you think?'

'I don't know.'

He just shook his head, as though it was obvious. 'Haven't had my dinner, for one thing,' he shouted, a minute later.

'No, me neither.'

'And Comrade Colonel says he won't be long. Well . . . we'll see about that.'

'Keeps you waiting, does he?'

'What do you think?'

I laughed. 'I wouldn't know.'

'Still,' he said, 'at least it's not all night.'

'No.'

'Not all night, every night.'

'No.'

'I don't know how I survived that summer,' he said.

He meant the summer of thirty-seven, when we worked all night, every night. The summer of thirty-seven. So much has been said about it. To understand what happened, we must start two and a half years earlier with the murder of Sergei Mironovich Kirov. Everyone, so they say, knows what they were doing when they heard the news of Kirov's murder. I had only been with the NKVD for a few months. It was 2 December 1934 — a freezing morning, the windows of the trams thick with ice and luminous in the dark — and I arrived at work as usual. I went into the office and took off my coat and hat. When the door opened a minute later, I expected it to be Ablamov. It was Pervukhin. 'Good morning, Comrade Colonel,' I said. 'There's a meeting in the mess at eight o'clock,' he said. 'And tell Ablamov.' It was obvious that something serious had happened. Though the mess was full, it was very quiet. Reshetov entered with Pervukhin and some other senior officers. Immediately, there was silence. Reshetov had a short, whispered conversation with Pervukhin. 'Comrades,' he said suddenly in a loud voice, 'there's been a terrible tragedy. Politburo member Comrade Sergey Mironovich Kirov has been shot and killed, in Leningrad.'

That things had been allowed to reach such a point was said to be the fault of the NKVD. We were 'lackadaisical' and 'unvigilant'. We had failed to follow up obvious leads, and had ignored the testimony of informers. Important suspects had been freed without proper interrogation. 'Stronger leadership' was said to be needed. We were permanently under pressure from politicians and the press. In July thirty-six, the directors of several failing enterprises — the Urals Copper Mining Trust and a few others — were arrested. Then in September, Reshetov suddenly went. His place as head of the oblast NKVD was taken by Dmitriev. There was in fact a huge turnover of personnel at all levels, unfamiliar faces everywhere, and a number of new investigations were launched. A few months later two other members of the obkom, Fuks and Golovin, were arrested for fraud and false accounting. A middle manager — I've forgotten his name — testified against them. Golovin was second secretary of the obkom, and when he was arrested Kabakov wrote an article in the 'Urals Worker' in what was obviously an attempt to distance himself from the spreading scandal. It didn't work. Throughout the spring, more arrests were made, until, in the high summer of thirty-seven, Andrei Andreyevich Andreyev arrived in Sverdlovsk. He stayed for a week and while he was here, virtually the entire obkom — including Kabakov himself — was thrown out in a series of vociferous public meetings. For as long as he had been first secretary, Kabakov had perpetrated fraud and embezzlement on a massive scale. Worse, he had unjustly expelled thousands of honest party members, and handed party membership to many of his own supporters. Many of these people were not even Communists. They were swept out en masse while Andreyev was here.

All summer the purge went on. Something very strange was happening under the cloudless sky. There was a stunned, surreal atmosphere in the emptying offices. Many positions in the state, party and security services were suddenly vacant.

One day of that summer has particularly stuck in my mind. In the morning I was at work, opening letters to the former head of the oblast NKVD, Dmitriev. Most of these letters were from members of the public with information to pass on. One of them, however, was from the wife of an officer who had been arrested himself — he had known what Kabakov was doing, and had said nothing. Quite possibly he had been in his pay. The officer's name was Ivan Blyakhman, and his wife's letter asked if she would be able to take his things from his office. She listed them — his party documents, insurance papers, vacation permit, and so on. Though I had not known Blyakhman personally, I was touched by his wife's letter, and when I left work, I went to his empty office and found his papers still in a desk drawer. Even his hat was where he had left it. His address was on his party card. A street of wooden houses with the Iset at the end. There was no answer when I knocked on the door, so I spoke to one of the neighbours, who told me that Blyakhman's wife had been evicted. He said he did not know where she was, so I left her husband's things with him to pass on if he ever saw her again. Then I went to meet Irina. We had a picnic, and spent the afternoon lying half-asleep in the park. That evening we went to the theatre.

Ever since then I have wondered what happened to Bliakhman's wife. It is true that thirty-seven took innocent men and women

71

— perhaps she was one of the innocent, perhaps not. Yet it still left Rightists in place throughout the state and party organisations. Why did this happen? I don't know. I was not in a position to know. Perhaps we simply stopped short, lost our nerve, lacked the historical will to press home the purge. Epshteyn understood the importance of historical will. The New Economic Policy of the twenties he saw as a surrender to petit bourgeois elements of the peasantry, as a failure of nerve, which particularly infuriated and depressed him because, as he told us, all previous social revolutions had failed because they had paused, moderated, lost their nerve. When he spoke of the stubbornness of parts of the peasantry, I thought of my own father. He was truly, as Epshteyn said, petit bourgeois in his mentality. A true kulak — proud to be the pike who swallowed the carp, and intractable as the frozen winter soil. 'The world is strong like water,' he said, 'and stupid like a pig.' That was his philosophy. It still saddens me to think of it. Why did he not understand? He was a victim of history. And history was his victim too. If instead of stubbornly obstructing he, and millions like him, had joined willingly in what had to be done, innumerable lives would have been saved. As it was, their stubbornness led to strikes and violence in the cities, where the food shortages were severe, and forced Lenin to introduce the NEP. And this would stay in place, and Epshteyn would fulminate against it, until the end of the decade, when the problem of the kulaks would be dealt with once and for all, as he had always insisted that it should be.

Communism is not violent. It is humane. To say that Communism is humane is to state the obvious, is self-evident. However, for Communism to be humane, it is first necessary to liquidate those elements that are implacably hostile to it, and since they will fight to preserve themselves and their social order — and why would they not? — this will inevitably involve violence. Epshteyn knew this very well. He had fought, and lost his arm, in the Civil War, and the flat left sleeve of his jacket might have been the subject of mockery. Other teachers were shown no mercy. For some reason, however, there was never any question of mocking Epshteyn, or even of mentioning it, unless he mentioned it first — which he sometimes did, with wry humour. He was tough, soldierly and erudite. We imitated his simple, emphatic way of speaking, the words he used, his way of smoking, of lighting a match with one hand. This was especially true of the more intellectually-minded of us in our final years at the school — the 'Epshteynites' as we were jokingly known. He impressed on us that even after victory in the Civil War, the Revolution was unfinished, that in fact the struggle for a more just world had hardly begun, and that it would be for us to ensure that it was seen through.

On Monday I went to see Gasselblat, head of the health secretariat of the oblispolkom. His office was on 1905 Square. He himself was middle-aged and nervous. He had a stutter. I told him that there was a man, Mikhail Naumovich Lozovsky, the director of a small hospital and medical institute, who had been identified as a security threat and should be moved. Gasselblat nodded. He wrote down the words 'Lozovsky' and 'Metelyev Log'. 'Understood,' he said.

I suggested Dyomkin as a suitable successor, 'though of course that's up to you.'

'Of course.'

I thanked him and left. When I got back to the office, I phoned Mikhalkov and told him what had happened. 'Fine,' he said. 'Well done.' And that seemed to be that. Unfortunately, it wasn't. A few days later Gasselblat phoned me. He said, 'Listen, there's been a p — , a p — , a problem.'

'What problem?'

The problem, he said, was that Lozovsky's post at Metelyev Log was on the nomenklatura. This was surprising — it seemed a very minor, unimportant post to be on the list. What it meant, of course, was that it was not possible to move Lozovsky without the say-so of the obkom.

'Well,' I said, impatiently, 'have you spoken to them?'

'Yes.'

'And?'

'First they said, 'Fine, fine.' Then I didn't hear from them for a few days. And when I phoned them this morning, to find out what was happening, they said I should just leave it. I don't know,' he said sadly. 'Maybe you should speak to them.'

When I told Mikhalkov, he was impatient, irritated. 'What's the problem?' he said. 'Why won't they move him?'

'I'm not sure.'

'Well have you spoken to them?'

I told him I hadn't.

'Why not?'

I said that I didn't know who I should speak to.

He sighed, unimpressed. An hour later, he phoned me back. 'Suvorov,' he said. 'Speak to Suvorov.'

'Suvorov?'

When he hung up, I sat there for a few moments staring at the phone. I had hoped he would speak to the obkom himself. It was an intimidating thing for me, for someone in my position, to have to do.

7

'He's with me,' Ivan says to the old man with the nicotine-stained forelock, suited like an undertaker, on the entrance of the First Department of the Turkish baths. Aleksandr no longer has access to the First Department except when Ivan signs him in. The old man waves them through with his cigarette and they start up the wide wheaten marble stairs. 'How's things?' Ivan says. 'Over the disappointment of the football yet?'

'I think so.'

'It wasn't just that we lost. It was the way we . . . ' He stops, in mid-sentence, to talk to someone on their way down — a man in late middle age with a heavy, sensuous face and very short grey hair. Ivan is not obsequious, not at all. However, he is highly, suavely solicitous. And he does all the smiling. The other man does not smile. Aleksandr, who stopped several steps up from them, is only able to hear snatches of their talk.

'Do you know who that was?' Ivan whispers, joining him.

'No.'

'Kantorovich.' Still in a whisper.

'Who's Kantorovich?' Not in a whisper.

Ivan looks quickly over his shoulder. 'Colonel-General Kantorovich,' he says in a low voice. 'Strategic rocket forces. Took part in the arms-limitation talks in Moscow last month. Met Nixon.'

'Oh yes?'

'Yes.'

'Proud of that, is he?'

'I think so. I would be.'

'What, of meeting Nixon?'

'No, of taking part in the talks. Not that it wouldn't be interesting to meet Nixon.'

They undress in the panelled warmth of the *predbannik*, the locker-room, and then proceed to the low light of the *banya*, where men, mostly middle-aged or older, sit or sprawl saggily on the wood shelves, some wearing wet flannel hats and mittens, otherwise naked, shining with sweat, flicking the sweat out of their eyes. No one speaks in the *banya*. The heat there is too intense for idle talk. There are only occasional short sighs. Aleksandr watches the drops of sweat slide over the sphere of his belly, the sweat-beaded backs of his hands. Yes, he thinks, *we have surrendered. Surrendered on Berlin, on Germany, on our strategic rocket forces, on everything. The surrender started with Khrushchev, of course. When*

Khrushchev took power, he immediately put in place policies which he knew would undermine the Soviet system. Why was he not stopped? Simple. He knew that only the MGB had the power to stop him, so his first step was to neutralise the MGB, the whole state security system. In this, he had the support of the many Rightists who were still in senior positions in the state and party structures — men who had not been liquidated in thirty-seven or later, and who had long been waiting for their moment to seize power. What they wanted was a change of political course — an abandonment of Marx's ideal of a society in which the wholeness of every human life is fulfilled. Loss of idealism. Yes. Idealism was lost, leaving nothing. Khrushchev's peasant materialism. Brezhnev's militarism. In the end we lost. Lost the ideal of moving towards Communism. In people's minds. That was the essential thing. To move towards it in people's minds. We did not work hard enough to do that. So the Rightists won, and 1937 did not destroy them. They were the people who supported Khrushchev, the people we failed to liquidate in the thirties and forties . . .

They stay in the *banya* for ten or twelve minutes, no more, and even then Ivan is a little light-headed when they emerge. 'Might have overdone it today,' he says, though they were in there for no longer than usual. The showers are simply huge spigots, with old-fashioned wooden handles, from which pours water, icy or piping hot.

Grisha, one of the *predbannik* attendants, a teenager, has been sent out for vodka. While they wait for him, they eat pork fat, smoked fish and bread. Someone is talking about football, about Yerevan, the first-division team. 'They play like Europeans,' he is saying. 'They're individualists. They'll shout at the ref if they don't agree with him . . . ' Someone else — he must be fiftyish, with flaccid muscles and a handlebar moustache — is telling a joke. 'Igor says to Yegor, 'You know what, I think my wife might be cheating on me.' 'Oh yeah,' Yegor says. 'Who with?' 'A florist.' 'What makes you think that?' 'Because when I got home unexpectedly the other day, I found this rose on the table.' 'Right.' So Yegor thinks for a minute, then he says, 'You know what? I think *my* wife might be cheating on me too.' 'Yeah?' Igor says. 'Who with?' 'A fella that works on the railway.' 'What makes you think that?' 'Well, when I got home unexpectedly the other day, I found her in bed with a fella that works on the railway.' ' Laughter. The joke-teller looks pleased with himself. He has numerous tattoos. Prominent on one shoulder is 'STALIN', on the other 'LENIN'. Nodding towards these with an ironic smile, Ivan says, 'Like the tattoos.' The joke-teller stares at him menacingly. Everyone laughs. 'Yeah, well.' He shrugs, inspecting himself. 'They were fashionable once, but now . . . You know . . . ' More laughter. Someone says, 'In the West they do tattoos without needlework. That's what I heard. They just sort of stamp them on you.'

When Grisha arrives with the vodka they let him have a shot, and he sits there sniffing it. His long hair comes down over the filthy collar of his jacket, and its lapels are covered with pins — presents from tourists, mostly from the fraternal nations, whom he met while working in a Crimean spa open to foreigners. He's most proud of one a Canadian woman gave him, a little red-and-white Canadian flag. He says he'd like to go to Canada, France and Japan. He says in those countries everyone has their own car, even ordinary workers. 'Well, I don't know about France or Canada,' Ivan says, 'but Japan . . . '

Aleksandr has heard what follows innumerable times. To listen to Ivan, he thinks, opening his locker, you would suppose that he had lived in Japan for twenty years, not spent two heavily supervised weeks in suburban Tokyo, shuttling to and from his hotel and the Olympic stadium. Grisha, however, is obviously impressed. So are some of the others. Soon, in fact, everyone is listening to Ivan. He says that yes, the streets are filled with cars — and what cars! Of course, he points out sternly to Grisha, Japan is a vassal state of the USA, and as such not to be envied — he offers him a Golden Fleece, which Grisha timidly takes — but what cars! They start first time, travel smoothly, never stall or judder or squeak. They are spacious and fragrant. And so many of them! The Soviet Union, he says, must learn to make such cars.

8

If you have forgotten this, Ivan, let me jog your memory — it is a summer night in 1948. I am knocking on the door of your mistress's flat. The stair-well smells of sewage. And the situation with Lozovsky is in a sort of stalemate. Suvorov, that odious obkom weasel, has said that he will not move him from his post. Suvorov — I don't know if you know this, Ivan — Suvorov turned out to be an old university pal of Lozovsky's. Sitting at his desk in his natty striped suit, smoking a foreign cigarette, he said to me, 'Yes, we knew each other in the twenties.' And he smiled his moustachioed smile. 'Several lifetimes ago. I wasn't in his league of course. He's an extraordinary talent. Extraordinary!' The showy smile. 'I'm not — I went into politics.' He thought that was very funny.

I said, 'You've known each other since then, since the twenties?'

He stopped smiling. 'No, no, not exactly. We were friends at university. Then we lost touch. I ended up here. He stayed in Moscow, of course. Sometimes I saw his picture in the papers. When he won the Stalin prize, for instance.'

'And then?'

'Then, well, then he and his wife moved out here, with the university. In forty-one . . . ' In forty-one, as the Nazis sliced through our western districts, Moscow University was evacuated to Sverdlovsk. 'We saw them socially, my wife and I,' Suvorov went on, 'until they moved to . . . ' He smiled and shook his head. 'I forget the name . . . '

'Metelyev Log.'

'Yes. When was it? Forty-four?'

There was a small wooden box on his desk which he opened — it was full of foreign cigarettes, as fat and white as maggots. He offered me one — 'No, thank you' — then lit one himself, with a silver lighter. 'In fact I tried to dissuade him from taking that job,' he said, in a puff of smoke. 'He wouldn't listen.'

Why not?

'He wanted it. He specifically asked for it.'

Why did he want it?

'I don't know.'

'You must have asked him,' I said politely. 'If you tried to dissuade him from taking it.'

'It doesn't mean I got an answer!' The smile faded. He shrugged. 'I imagine it was to focus on his work,' he said. 'His scientific work. He felt he had a unique opportunity. He said that.

84

Or something like that.'
'A unique opportunity?'
'Yes, a unique opportunity.'
'What did he mean by that?'
'You know,' Suvorov said, 'I have no idea.'
And since then, since Lozovsky moved to Metelyev Log, had he seen much of him?
He stuck out his lower lip and shook his head. 'No,' he said. 'Not much.' This seemed straightforward enough, until I asked him when he had last seen or spoken to Lozovsky. 'Well . . . ' he said. 'On Monday.'
'Monday? This Monday?'
'Yes.'
Now somewhat wary, Suvorov said, 'Yes, I spoke to him on Monday. On the telephone.'
And what had he wanted?
He had wanted to warn his old friend, now a senior member of the obkom, that there might be a move to ease him out of his post at Metelyev Log, and that he did not want to be eased out of it, and that whatever story Suvorov might hear from the MGB, the reason they wanted him out was that he had not signed a form four-eighty in respect of one of his patients, and that he had not signed it for perfectly valid medical reasons. 'And if that's the case,' Suvorov said, with a sad smile, 'I don't see what you want me to do.'
Mikhalkov took this unexpected move of

Lozovsky's personally. He was furious, and the immediate target of his fury was me. Why had I made such a mess of this simple task? Why didn't I just do what he wanted? Why did I always find some new problem? I stood in his office, staring at the blue carpet. I was surprised how strongly he felt about the situation. I did not fully understand its importance to him. What was obvious was that Lozovsky had not signed the form because he did not think he needed to; he knew that he was on the nomenklatura, and that through his friend Suvorov the obkom would obstruct our efforts to move him.

For a week or two I heard no more about it. Then, one afternoon, I was summoned to Mikhalkov's office.

'You've got a journalist brother, haven't you?' he said.

'Yes.'

'I want you to have a word with him.'

And that is why I found myself trudging up the stairs to your mistress's flat, Ivan. I've forgotten her name. Perhaps you have too. When I went to your flat, Katya told me that you were working late. Her face shone with sweat, and she was fanning herself with a folded newspaper. 'And you — are you well?' I said. 'You shouldn't smoke, you know.' She let me take the papirosa from her hand. 'You should look after yourself.' I left, feeling implicated in your lies to her. I did not look for you at the newspaper offices. I knew I wouldn't find you there.

I said to you, 'Your wife's eight months pregnant. Don't you think you should be with her?' I didn't keep my voice down. I wanted your mistress and her neighbours to hear.

And you said, 'It's not your business. What do you want?'

We went outside and spoke in the street. It was a moonless night. A hundred metres away tall pale lights marked the intersection. Mosquitoes tormented us. And I told you there was a piece I thought you should write for the newspaper.

'What piece?' you said.

'Something important.'

'What?' You were still irritable, and slightly suspicious.

I explained the situation to you. Not the situation with Lozovsky, of course. Not him specifically. The wider situation. You listened in silence. Negative foreign influences, I said, were starting to pervade the intellectual life of the Soviet Union. Nihilistic influences. Even in the sciences. Yes, even in the sciences. For an example one might point to the work of an eminent neuropsychologist living in Sverdlovsk oblast, Mikhail Naumovich Lozovsky . . .

And you said, 'It's not my sort of thing, Sasha.'

'Let me finish. Mikhail Naumovich Lozovsky, who thinks the world is inherently meaningless. That meaning is a purely subjective phenomenon. He has written this, in scientific journals . . . '

This was true. Lozovsky had written that, in so many words. It was what Mikhalkov had found — a piece in a scientific journal, published in 1936.

'Sasha,' you said, 'it's not my thing.'

'Do you understand what I'm saying?'

'It's not my thing, Sasha.'

'Why not?'

'It's just not. I don't know anything about it.'

As if that had ever stopped you in the past!

'Don't worry about that,' I said. 'I have some material for you.'

'What material?'

'About Lozovsky.'

'What do you mean? What sort of material?'

'Material. Facts.'

'Facts?'

'Of course. This is important,' I said. 'It's going to be an important piece.'

You sighed. 'Would I be able to speak to him?'

'Lozovsky? No.'

'Why not?'

'Vanya . . . '

'Why wouldn't I be able to speak to him?' You were petulant now.

'Why do you need to speak to him? This is going to be an important piece, Vanya. Do you understand? What have you been working on? Interviewing Stakhanovites?' That was what you did in those days, Ivan. You interviewed Stakhanovites. 'Aleksey Tishchenko, along with his wife Zoya, arrived in Sverdlovsk in 1945 with all their possessions in a single suitcase made of newspaper. Now, only three years later, the couple own furniture, including a couch and a wardrobe . . . ' You know the sort of thing. 'That must get pretty tedious,' I said. 'They're all the same aren't they, Stakhano-vites . . . '

I think what I was saying must have upset you. I think that's why you suddenly said, 'I wrote that thing I told you about.'

'What thing?'

'The strike. You know.'

There was a long silence. 'You wrote it?' You said nothing. 'Why? WHY? I told you not to!'

'I know — '

'Why did you write it? Why did you do that? Don't you understand?'

'I understand — '

'No, you don't! What was the point? The piece wasn't published. You've got to think.

You've got a family now. What if you lose your job? What did your editor say?'

'Nothing.'

'Nothing? He's said nothing to you about it?'

'No.'

You seemed to think this was a positive sign. You were wrong. I said so. And then I said, 'I have to tell you, Ivan, it would be in your interests to write this piece, the Lozovsky piece.'

'What do you mean?' you said sharply.

'I'm not threatening you.' I was upset that you had misunderstood me. I found your shoulder in the night. I was almost in tears. You may not have seen it, but you must have heard it in my voice. 'Of course I'm not threatening you. I'm worried about you. The sort of name you're making for yourself. Once you start to make that sort of name . . . You know what I'm talking about. This is an opportunity for you. That's all I'm saying. Think about it. Please.'

You did know what I was talking about, and you did think about it. The tall pale lights of the intersection, a hundred metres off, stood in a snowstorm of insects.

'Why do you want it?' you said.

'Why do I want it?'

'Yes, why do you want it?'

'What difference does it make?'

'I want to know.'

'Vanya . . . '

'If I do it, I want to know. Why?'

When I said nothing, you sighed and said, 'I'm tired, Sasha . . . '

'They want Lozovsky out of his job.'

'Who does? Why?'

'What does it matter? It's politics. They want him out. The obkom's stuck its heels in. There's a friend of his, something . . . It's not very edifying. They want to get this material out. You don't have to worry about that though. The story itself is totally sound. It's not even about Lozovsky. Forget Lozovsky. He's just an example of a wider phenomenon. That's what the story's about, and it's very important.'

★ ★ ★

Your piece appeared on the front page of the 'Urals Worker' a week later. When you submitted it, the editor, not knowing what to do, phoned Mikhalkov — you yourself had told him to do this — and Mikhalkov, pretending to be unsure how to proceed, had pointed him to Veklishev. Having heard from the editor, Veklishev then phoned Mikhalkov with the name 'Lozovsky' and asked him who this was. Mikhalkov said he would look into it, and twenty-four hours later told Veklishev that he had looked into it, and found some quite worrying things. The unpublished newspaper piece seemed 'spot on', and in view of this, Mikhalkov said, it might be wise to move Lozovsky from 'such a sensitive post'. One of Veklishev's secretaries phoned the editor and two days later your piece was published. That weekend Veklishev went duck-shooting with Shestakov, who was then first secretary of the obkom. He mentioned the subject to him, and Shestakov — who had seen the story on the front page of the newspaper — said he would take it up with Suvorov, which he did. And ordered him to move Lozovsky from his post. Mikhalkov was all smiles.

Then the telegram from Moscow.

This was not expected. It took even Mikhalkov by surprise. 'We got this today,' he said, passing it to me. 'Article 58.' I.e. 'Propaganda or agitation, containing an appeal for the overthrow, subverting or weakening of the Soviet power, and equally the dissemination or preparation or possession of literary materials of similar content.' 'I suppose they read the 'Urals Worker' in Moscow,' he said. 'Surprising as that may seem.'

I did not smile at this. I said nothing.

The next day I went to the procuracy, and took a number, and waited until a tired-looking official summoned me into his office, which was unpleasantly stuffy. The official — a stout old woman of a middle-aged man with a small moustache, and large patches of sweat in the armpits of his shirt — opened the window, and asked me to give him a short — he stressed the word 'short' — summary of the indictment. When I had finished, he went through the warrant line by line. Then he stamped it. We arrested Lozovsky the following week, when he was in town for a meeting at the oblispolkom.

9

Summer has burned itself out in dust and yellow grass. Unseen, weightless, its dead insects accumulate under the furniture. The Icelandic police will soon make their report. They have spent the night searching the Laugardalshöll Sports Exhibition Palace — dismantling furniture, probing wall cavities, prising up floorboards. Searching for electronic devices. Yesterday, Yefim Geller — Spassky's second — made a public statement in which he accused the Americans of using such devices to interfere with Boris Vasilyevich's brain. Members of the American delegation, he said, were often to be found in the hall when chess was not being played.

And something is evidently wrong with Boris Vasilyevich's brain. In photographs he looks haunted and hollow-eyed. Sleepless. Profoundly troubled.

Following Fischer's extraordinary error, he won the first game, and Fischer did not even turn up for the second, thus forfeiting it. 2-0, and it was Fischer, not Boris Vasilyevich, who seemed to be psychologically disintegrating. Only a long, pleading phone-call from Henry

Kissinger, it is said, prevented him from leaving Iceland.

In very strange circumstances, however, Fischer won the next game. It was played, at his insistence, in a small, stuffy room normally used for table tennis.

Once more in the main hall, the fourth game was drawn, though Boris Vasilyevich should probably have won it, and his failure to do so was ominous. Especially when Fischer won the next two games to take the overall lead. In the second of these games, he took Spassky totally by surprise by opening with d4. It was the first time in his life that Fischer had opened with anything other than e4. Spassky seemed stunned, shocked, unable to think straight, and was torn to shreds. And when, following this, he stood and joined in the applause, Aleksandr, listening in Sverdlovsk, wept at his magnanimity, and knew in his heart that the match was over. Two games later, Fischer extended his lead to 4-2.

Pleading 'illness', Spassky then took a few days off. Then he played a sad, desultory draw. He was in distress. When he lost the tenth game, it was even suggested in Moscow that the match might be stopped. Boris Vasilyevich himself insisted on playing on. His psychological problems seemed so severe that it surprised everyone when he won the eleventh game. The twelfth was a tense stalemate. Fischer won the next, and four more draws followed. Then Yefim Geller made his intervention, and the Icelandic police went in.

Very solemnly, they are making their report. Aleksandr turns up the volume. They say that they have found . . . no electronic devices. They have found nothing — nothing except, in one of the lighting fixtures . . . two dead flies. They invite the US and Soviet delegations to examine these flies . . .

He switches off the radio.

Of course there were no electronic devices. You do not need electronic devices to interfere with someone's brain. Fischer has been interfering very effectively with poor Boris Vasilyevich's brain for a month and a half without them. His insistence that the third game be played in the table-tennis room was the turning point. The room was not adequately soundproofed and street noise filtered in — Spassky's people blamed his defeat on that. But it was not the street noise in itself that upset Boris Vasilyevich. It was Fischer. Since then, it has not been a matter of sport so much as pure psychological warfare, something to which Fischer's particular type of egomania lends itself well. To be fair-minded, however, to be honest and straightforward, is an insupportable weakness. And Boris Vasilyevich is unquestionably all of those things.

Aleksandr sits down on the sofa. There is a tingle in the hinterland of his nose, his throat is tight. It will be the first time since 1948 that the world chess champion is not a citizen of the Soviet Union; then, the FIDE tournament in Moscow was won by Mikhail Botvinnik — he was not even a professional chessplayer; he was a Soviet engineer. A sober proletarian. A Stalinist, and as steely as poor Spassky is soft.

★   ★   ★

The next morning he takes a tram to the Rastorguyev-Kharitonov Park. Empty on a weekday afternoon in early autumn — the last week of August, and suddenly there is an autumnal tone to things — it is still substantially the same as it was in 1948. The man-made lake echoing the monochrome sky, the white rotunda on the island. The trees starting to lose their leaves. It has been years since he has seen the place. He stops on the path near the water's edge. The surface of the lake is a green so dark it is almost black; further out, the inverted world of sky and encircling trees. Was it here, on this spot, that it happened? Somewhere near here. There is no sign of it now. The place has taken no imprint from the event. He stands there for a minute — an observer might think he had lost something — and then walks on. Making his way under the trees, he finds the place where the Pobeda was parked. There are new buildings in the street, and the trees are very much larger than they were. They were small then, little more than saplings; and as slowly as the hour hand of a watch, their shadows moved. Lieutenant Ivanov started the engine and trundled the Pobeda forward until it was once more immersed in them. He turned the key. The engine hiccuped, whimpered, was silent.

Squinting out at the park, Aleksandr was aware of Ivanov's halitosis — a surprisingly faecal smell — as he exhaled in the seat next to him. Their shoulders were more or less touching. Snapping out of momentary sleeps, he would find the sunlit park still there, the quivering shouts, Lieutenant Voronin's floating papirosa smoke. He felt sick. He had felt sick since the previous evening.

Irina had found him lying on the divan. It was still light outside, though the room was starting to fill with shadows. 'Are you alright?' she said.

'No. I feel sick.'

'Do you?'

She started to unpack their weekly parcel from the Ministry of State Security supply store. If she seemed unsympathetic it was because they had had a fight twenty-four hours earlier and had not spoken since. In the middle of the shouting he had just left and walked the streets for an hour. Though it was eight o'clock the sun was still high in the sky. He mounted the stairs in the huge stairwell, which smelled of damp plaster even in summer, and let himself into the flat. Zalesky's family had vacated the kitchen. Though he had not eaten all day, he was not hungry. On the floor next to the divan was a seashell with two cigarette-ends in it — Irina had smoked, and now she was asleep. Standing there in the dim silence, he looked at her inert face. It looked ugly and pallid. Her small mouth was slightly open, and there were purple shadows under her brown eyelids. Her dry hair was spread out on the stained pillow. Her thin arms were pulled up protectively in front of her . . .

She finished unpacking the supply parcel, and put the soap to one side. 'Was it something you ate?' she said.

'Probably.'

'What?'

'I don't know.'

'If it was, it must have been something you ate at work.' She sat on the edge of the divan and put her hand on his forehead. 'You don't have a fever,' she said.

'No.'

'I'm sure it's nothing. You'll feel better tomorrow.'

He would not.

The interior of the Pobeda was infused with the smell of sweat, like an old shirt — the leather, the stained ticking, even the wood. Voronin was reading something out from the newspaper. A feature on Polina Gelman. Voronin was obsessed with Polina Gelman. He said the idea of a female fighter pilot excited him, 'especially a Jewess'. When he had finished the feature, he turned the page. '*The overthrow of British imperialism in Palestine,*' he said in his nasal voice, '*and the establishment there of the state of Israel, should be seen as a progressive development, supportive of the international socialist movement. It occurred with the full support of the newly formed Communist Party of Israel (previously the Palestine Communist Party), which is a leading force in the new government. The Soviet Union has recognised the state of Israel, and calls on all countries in the region to respect UN Security Council resolution 181, which partitions Palestine into two states . . .* '

In the twilight, Irina stood up and started to prepare her supper. 'Maybe you should eat something,' she said. 'Have you eaten anything today?'

'No.'

'Maybe you should eat something then.'

'I'm not hungry.'

'Have you actually been throwing up?'

'Not really.'

When she opened a tin of processed meat, he shut his eyes and turned to face the wall.

He slept for a while.

When he woke he lay on the divan watching Irina undress; her pale yellowish skin, her elegant shoulders — she was proud of her shoulders — the folded plumpness of her belly, the fine somewhat scant hair pressed flat by her underwear. It struck him as sad that watching her he experienced no more than a vague, wavering desire. He knew that there were many men — Lieutenant Morozov, who lived downstairs, for one — who would envy his lying there, watching Irina undress in the twilight; for whom it would be an exciting, almost a fantastical experience. Quite possibly, Morozov was lying downstairs imagining it at that very moment — hearing through his open window the same sounds that Aleksandr was hearing (the donkey cart passing outside in the street, the whisper of the wheels, the quick tapping of the little hooves) — and imagining with a sort of yearning pain what Aleksandr was actually seeing. And seeing it, he experienced only this vague, wavering desire, which seemed little more than the memory of a former desire. If he had wanted to he might have stood up and taken two steps through the twilight and touched her — touched her hips, her thighs, her lips — as Morozov so painfully longed to, and never would. Her lingering there seemed a sort of invitation. Though his pulse had quickened perceptibly, however, he did not move.

And in fact Irina did not seem aware that he was watching her. Moving quickly and efficiently, she wrapped her hair up in a stiff towel, took off her watch, and shouldered on her dressing-gown. Then she went, and in the sudden stillness he saw the soap, still where she had left it by the door — presumably so that she would not forget it — and wondered whether to take it to her. He was about to do this, or had decided that he should, when the door opened impatiently and she snatched it herself.

He had fallen into a light sleep and was woken by the sound of the door shutting. It was nightfall. He felt feverish, and hoped only that he would sleep until morning. He was sweating under the single sheet. Irina lit the special little oil-lamp that was supposed to ward off mosquitoes. Her hair was loose, making a wet patch on her dressing gown. She stepped out of her slippers and went to the window, where there was still some pale light, and started to brush her hair.

When she had finished she sat down on the divan. Feeling the pressure of her weight on the old springs, he opened his eyes. It was almost dark. She was looking down at him.

'What?' he murmured.

'How are you feeling?' She smelled of soap, was still warm from her bath.

He shook his head.

'You'll feel better tomorrow.'

Her dressing gown was loosely tied and from where he lay he was able to see the pale profile of her left breast inside it. He put out his hand and touched it, felt the infinite softness of its tip in his palm. She turned slightly from the waist to move it towards him. Eventually he withdrew his hand, and shut his eyes, and she leaned over and kissed him.

Though he then fell asleep, he did not sleep through to the morning. He fell asleep while she smoked a cigarette sitting in the not-quite-night. There had been something peaceful about that — the tiny sounds of her smoking, the scent of the smoke itself — and imagining the tumbling rush of the water through the sluice gates of the Plotinka, he had slipped quietly into sleep.

When first aware, some hours later, that he was awake, he did not open his eyes or move his limbs from where they were. He stayed perfectly still. However he was too hot. The sheet was wet with his sweat. The frogs were singing in the street. He hoped it was almost morning. It was midnight.

10

We waited for Lozovsky in an old Pobeda in the shade of some trees on the edge of the Rastorguyev-Kharitonov Park. He would have to pass through the park on his way to the station. We expected him at one o'clock. When he still wasn't there at two, I sent Voronin to find out what was happening. 'Are you alright?' I said, turning in my seat to face him. He nodded, fiddling with a wet handkerchief. 'Should you be smoking?'

'S'alright . . . ' He sneezed.

'Why do you keep sneezing?'

'It's the p — ' he said, into another sneeze. 'It's the pollen. These trees . . . '

'I want you to find a phone and find out what's happened to Lozovsky.'

'A phone?'

'Yes.'

'Where?'

'I don't know. Find one.'

'What should I say?'

'Just find out what's happened to him, whether he's left. Maybe he stayed for lunch. I don't know.'

Voronin wandered off down the street.

I was starting to worry. Lozovsky was supposed to have spent the morning in meetings at the oblispolkom. No mention would have been made of Yudin. He would have talked small talk with the health service managers, Gasselblat and his ilk, perhaps eaten a plain lunch, and left. And if he had been nervous when he arrived in Sverdlovsk the previous evening — it was his first visit to town since his refusal to sign the form — the way in which everything passed off normally would surely have made him feel more secure, probably more secure than he had felt for weeks. So where was he? Had we missed him somehow? The thought made me very tense. An hour earlier, I had been nervous about seeing Lozovsky — it was an unfortunate, unpleasant situation. Now I just wanted him to show up. And I was not well. When I looked at the park it seemed to seethe. I scanned the slope on the far side for Afanasyev. When Lozovsky showed up, Afanasyev was supposed to speak to him, to say that he knew him. (He was about Lozovsky's age, though still a lieutenant.) He was then supposed to walk him towards the place where the Pobeda was parked in the shade. When they were near, Ivanov and Voronin would get out. However Afanasyev seemed to have fallen asleep. 'I think Afanasyev's fallen asleep,' I said. Ivanov was standing next to the car in his shirtsleeves, smoking a cigarette. I was about to tell him to go over there and wake him, when Afanasyev sat up. For a few moments he looked around as though wondering where he was. Then he slowly got to his feet. He looked at his watch. 'What's he doing?' I said.

We watched as Afanasyev started to walk away. He was walking towards the trees, where there was a little tea shop, the Orangery, in an old Palladian pavilion. Minutes passed. I waited with my eyes on the point where Afanasyev had vanished into the shade under the trees. In my feverish state, I felt the situation slipping away from me. Finally I said to Ivanov, 'Wait here. I'll be back in a minute.'

I took Afanasyev's attitude personally — he was twelve years older than I was, and seemed to feel this entitled him to ignore my orders. Though I felt light-headed, I started to jog through the shade under the trees, towards the sun-dappled façade of the Orangery. In front of it there was a small formal garden, and there, in spite of everything, I was struck by the fact that in one of the parterres the gardeners had made a portrait of the First Secretary of the party out of plants, entirely in shades of green. It was extraordinarily well done. I was still staring at it when I noticed that something unusual seemed to be happening in the

107

Orangery. People were standing in the entrance, trying to see inside. I told them to move, and went in. There were many more people inside, in the strange, creamy light. In spite of this, it was very quiet. 'What is it?' I said. 'What's the matter? What's happened?' At first there was silence, then someone said, 'It was a heart attack.' And someone else: 'No, not a heart attack.'

'Who?'

Afanasyev, of course.

He lay on the tiled floor, with his head propped on something, perhaps his jacket. His face was ashen. Someone had loosened his tie. The light fell from above, through the filthy, orange, translucent dome. He seemed unconscious. I was immediately sorry that I had been so furious, that I had made the poor old fellow sit for over two hours in the sun. He looked so helpless, so stricken — a forty-eight-year-old lieutenant. A man who in twenty-eight years of service had risen from junior lieutenant to senior lieutenant. His chin shone with saliva, his grey moustache looked wet. 'Has someone called an ambulance?' I said.

A strange silence had fallen in the Orangery. Probably they had found Afanasyev's Ministry of State Security card in his jacket pocket. They parted to let me through, and I squatted down next to his head. If he was aware of me at all, it seemed unlikely that he knew who I was. I put my hand on his shoulder — his shirt was literally sodden — and said, 'You're going to be okay, Afanasyev.' I don't know why I used his surname. 'You're going to be okay,' I said in a whisper. And for a minute I stayed there, with my hand on his wet shoulder.

My eyes started to wander nervously — on the nearest table there was a newspaper, an untouched tea with a segment of lemon suspended in it. Further off, three dusty pot plants stood awkwardly under the little dome. I felt the cool grittiness of the tiled floor under my palm.

Afanasyev was shivering. 'Put his jacket over him,' I said. A woman placed it over his torso. 'When was the ambulance called?'

Someone said, 'Ten minutes ago?'

I squeezed Afanasyev's shoulder and stood up.

The standing heat, the looser noises of outside, struck me as I stepped out of the Orangery. It was half past two — I had been in there for only a few minutes. Making my way towards the place where the Pobeda was parked, I felt feverish and did not notice Ivanov until I was quite near him. The park was full. There were people everywhere. Ivanov was standing on the path near the water's edge. He had his pistol in his hand. When I saw that all sound seemed to fall away. There was a man in a linen suit and a panama, walking towards Ivanov. I was not sure it was Lozovsky until he stopped, and turned, and started to walk the other way, towards me. I thought I saw Ivanov lift his pistol. 'No!' I shouted. 'Don't shoot!' In his panic, Lozovsky seemed to push over a child, who started to scream. The child's mother was shouting at him. She snatched his sleeve and shook it, and it was then that he saw me. His mouth was open, he was panting slightly, his face had a sheen of perspiration. For a few moments the woman kept shouting at him. Then, sensing something intense about his silence, she stopped. 'Hello, Mikhail Naumovich,' I said, walking up to them, forcing myself to look him in the eye. I put my hand on his arm. 'I want a word with you.'

We left the park at a measured pace. People stepped off the path to let us pass. I was only vaguely aware of them. I had my hand on Lozovsky's arm, and was probably squeezing it tightly. He had still not said a word, and sat in the Pobeda as if he was expecting a lift home, innocently fanning himself with his panama. 'What's this about?' he said. I put my hand in my jacket pocket — I was not wearing my jacket; it was next to me on the seat — and pulled out the arrest warrant. He looked at it while Ivanov started the engine. 'What does this mean?' he said. 'Is it because I didn't sign that form?'

'No.'

'Why then?'

'I'm not supposed to say,' I said. 'It's something you wrote.'

'Something I wrote? What?'

I was aware of Ivanov listening from his seat in the front. He turned the Pobeda onto Karl Libknekht Street. 'Something you wrote in the thirties. In a scientific journal.'

'What thing?' Lozovsky was almost shouting. 'What scientific journal?'

'I'm sorry,' I said, turning to the window. 'I'm sorry.' I had a splitting headache, and was suddenly extremely sleepy. I just wanted to sleep.

It was not a long drive, only a few minutes. I left the paperwork to Ivanov and went to tell Mikhalkov what had happened. Then, on my way home, I went to the hospital to see how Afanasyev was. He seemed surprisingly well. 'What happened?' I said. 'What was it?'

'Diabetes.'

'Well . . . ' I said. 'That's not so bad. I was worried. I thought it was a heart attack or something.'

Afanasyev shook his head. 'No,' he said. 'Diabetes.'

111

* ★ ★

A few days after Lozovsky's arrest I went to Metelyev Log for the last time. I was looking through the books in his office — with one exception, they were medical textbooks in Russian, English and German — when there was a knock on the door. 'Yes!' I shouted. Sosnovsky put his head in. 'It's that bloke again,' he said. I was turning the pages of a huge volume — not merely written in German, but printed in Gothic script — and did not look up. 'What does he want?'

'He says he wants to talk to you,' Sosnovsky said.

'Okay.'

He opened the door a little wider. Entering the sunny room, Dyomkin looked at me shiftily. 'Where's Mikhail?' he said.

'Professor Lozovsky's not coming back.'

'Oh?'

'I've got this for you.' It was the letter offering him Lozovsky's job.

He looked quickly at the official envelope.

'Open it,' I said.

Frowning, he tore it open and pulled out Gasselblat's letter. I watched him as he read it. His face — he looked a little like Otto Schmidt, the polar explorer — was impassive. The letter did not, of course, explain what had happened

112

to Lozovsky. When he had finished, he looked up.

'So?' I said.

'So?'

'Will you take the job?'

He laughed. 'Do I have a choice?'

'Of course.'

There was a long pause. Then, with a shrug, he said, 'I'll take it.'

'Well . . . congratulations. When we've finished in here, you can move your stuff in.' He nodded, but did not move. He seemed unsure of himself — of the meaning of what had just happened, of what he should do. 'Oughtn't you to telegraph them,' I suggested, 'and let them know you're taking the job? The oblispolkom.' He stared at me for a moment, then turned to leave. 'And I'd like a word with you later, if you've got a minute.'

He did not acknowledge this immediately. First, with a sort of flourish, he opened the door. Then he said, 'For you, Major, I always have a minute.'

It was noon when I finished searching Lozovsky's office. I found only one thing of interest — a slim volume by a man named Nikolai Maksimovich Luzhov, which I took with me. Leaving Sosnovsky to watch things, Voronin and I left the hospital and set off down the forest track to the house. Ivanov and

Timashev were sitting on the wooden steps of the house laughing about something when we walked up to them. 'Everything alright?' I said.

Ivanov said, 'A woman was here. She wanted to go in. She said she lived here.'

'Did you let her?'

'No.'

'She was probably Lozovsky's wife.'

'She was.' Ivanov smiled. 'Wanted to know if we'd seen her husband.'

'What did you say?'

'I said we hadn't.'

'When was this?'

'An hour ago?'

'Do you know where she went?'

They shook their heads.

I knew the interior of the house well. It was low and small-windowed. Everything was wood, though variously hued — the floor, the walls, the furniture. Everything except the stove. When I touched it, it was very slightly warm. 'Okay,' I said to Voronin, who had followed me in. 'Let's start.'

We searched the living room, then went upstairs. The slatted, ladder-like steps emerged through the floor of a narrow space with a filthy window. The bedroom door was warped and would not shut properly. I had never been in there until then. There was a washstand and — something from a nineteenth-century

European town house — a large porcelain ewer. From the same sort of house there was a low-seated chair, upholstered in faded rose fabric. There were some women's underclothes on the chair. There was a pine chest with a large glass bottle on it, in which there were some dead flowers, their brown rotten stalks standing in discoloured water. On the wall was a small painting, in the Impressionist style, a sort of oil sketch, a view of a mountain lake.

I stood on the threshold for a few moments. Then I said to Voronin, 'You search this room. I'm going upstairs.'

He looked surprised. It would be more usual for me to search the suspect's room myself. Why didn't I? I'm not sure. There was a sense of trespass. It was very hot and I was sweating. I opened the filthy little window. Ivanov and Timashev were still sitting on the front steps. I shut the window and went downstairs, shouting to Voronin to hurry up.

★   ★   ★

Dyomkin took his time over the form four-eighty. I stood there in his office, waiting. 'Is this really necessary?' he said finally.

'Is what necessary?'

'This.' When I said nothing, he went on: 'I've seen Yudin. He's an imbecile. He can't even go

115

to the toilet on his own.'

'Sign it, please.'

He sighed and shook his head. Then he searched his desk for a pen. 'Well,' he said, when he found one, 'I'm sure you know what you're doing.' He shot me a sharp look, which he held for several seconds. Then he sighed again, noisily, and signed the form. 'There.' He threw down the pen.

'Thank you.'

'I get my huge new office now, do I?'

'If you want. It's up to you, isn't it.'

'Yes, it is. So.' He stood up. 'You off now?'

I nodded.

'Well . . . Say hello to Mikhail from me. If you see him. I'm sure you will.' I ignored this, and had opened the door when he said, 'You've not seen Nadezhda Filippovna, have you? Madame Lozovsky.'

'No, I haven't.'

'Does she know?'

'Probably,' I said.

'Probably? What — you mean she's probably put two and two together?'

'I don't know. What's it got to do with you?'

He smiled. 'Don't get upset!'

'I'm not upset . . . '

'I just want to know if I get to break the news to her, that's all.'

'If you want.'

116

'Not that I know anything, of course.'

He held my stare for a moment, then lowered his head to light a papirosa.

'I want Doctor Anichkova to travel with Yudin,' I said. 'If you can spare her.'

He looked at me vacantly for a few seconds. 'Fine,' he said.

'She'll be back tomorrow. Or the next day.'

'Fine.'

★ ★ ★

The men were lounging on the front steps of the hospital in their shirtsleeves. Joining them, I sat down in the shade on one of the stone steps. The afternoon was windless, the shaggy pines very still under the mountain sky. 'We'll have to go in two lots,' I said. 'I'll go first with Yudin and the doctor.' When the old Ford pulled up, however, it occurred to me that they might as well leave first, while I waited for Anichkova and Yudin.

When they had left, I stood up and walked down the steps into the sunshine. The hospital had a sadly dilapidated look. Weeds sprouted from its flaking off-white façade. Without Lozovsky and the prestige of his work it would no longer be possible to justify the expense of its existence, and it would shut. There was a sudden small splosh in the ornamental pond. I turned, and noticed a fringed shape of shiny black water on its green surface, where a frog had just plunged in. Sweating, the sun strong on my neck, I thought how wonderfully fresh the water must be, how green and secret the light under the surface mat of weed. Standing there on the paved edge of the pond, I was able to see a small part of my face mirrored — monochrome and ethereal — in the inky shape that the frog had made. With one eye shut and the other fixed on it, I moved my head slowly one way, then slowly the other.

While I was doing this, I was startled by a woman's voice.

I turned sharply, opening my left eye.

Lozovsky's wife, Nadezhda Filippovna, was standing there, squinting. I had not seen her since my first visit to Metelyev Log. When I was there for the second time, in May, I did not see her at all.

'Hello,' I said.

'I've just spoken to Maks,' she said, straight out, shielding her eyes with her hand. 'He says Mikhail's been arrested. Is it true?'

Surprised, I simply said, 'Yes.'

'He says it's because he didn't sign a form.'

'He's wrong.'

'Why then?' She stared at me for a few moments, from under her hand. 'What's going to happen to him?'

'I don't know.'

'Do you know where he is?'

'He's in Sverdlovsk.'

'Have you seen him?'

'I saw him a few days ago. He's okay.'

'And what . . . ' She seemed frustrated. 'What did he do? You don't know?'

'I'm sorry . . . '

'Were you in the house earlier?' she said suddenly.

'Yes.'

'Did you take my journal?'

'No.'

'Well, it isn't there.'

I said, 'One of my men may have taken it.'

'Do you need it?'

'I doubt it.'

'May I have it back then?'

I explained that it had already been taken to the station, and said I would see it was sent to her. 'What does it look like?' I said.

'It's . . . It's just a blue . . . It has a blue cover.'

'Okay.'

She seemed nervous. We stood there in the sunshine for a few moments. Then I said, 'This place will probably shut soon. Your friend Maks doesn't know, by the way.'

'He's not my friend.'

'Well . . . He doesn't know.'

119

I saw Anichkova step out into the portico at the top of the steps. We would be leaving in a few minutes.

'Do you have somewhere to stay?' I said. 'If this place does shut?' She looked surprised, said nothing. I said I might be able to find her somewhere in town, and wrote down my telephone number. I told her to phone me if she needed help. I felt I owed her this after what she and her husband had done for me when I was first at Metelyev Log. Anichkova, who had walked down the steps, was watching us with her arms folded. While she waited, she lit a papirosa, and immediately Nadezhda Filippovna turned to her and said, 'Sorry, would it be possible . . . ' Anichkova nodded, and offered her one. 'Thanks,' she said. I stood there while Anichkova lit it for her. Then, when it was lit, and without even looking at me, she went up the steps and inside.

11

The new Union of Journalists hunting lodge opens next month, and as one of the most senior members of the union in the *oblast*, Ivan expects to use it frequently. Listening to him extolling its luxuries, Aleksandr is reminded of a joke he overheard on the tram. It involves Brezhnev and his mother, who — in the joke — still lives in a peasant village. Brezhnev has invited her to his own hunting lodge in Zavidovo, and proudly shows her around — the panelled dining room, the swimming pool, the sunken bath, the forest stocked with deer and bear. 'Well, Mama,' he says, at the end of the tour. 'How do you like it?' 'It's marvellous!' she says. 'But aren't you afraid the Bolsheviks might come back?'

Aleksandr smiles to himself and Ivan stops speaking. 'What is it?'

'Nothing.'

Ivan looks at him quizzically for a moment. Then he presses on, telling them proudly about the modern bathhouse, the under-floor heating, the dining room panelled in Karelian pine. 'We'll all drive down there one weekend this autumn!' he says. 'We'll put a hunting party together. Shoot some duck. How about that, Shurik?'

Aleksandr Ivanovich smiles and shrugs. 'Sure . . . ' he says.

'When do you return to Leipzig, Aleksandr Ivanovich?' Spiridon enquires politely.

'End of September.'

'For your final year, is it?'

'M-hm.'

'And how do you like Germany?'

They are all in Ivan's flat to watch the opening ceremony of the Olympic Games on the colour television. Aleksandr Ivanovich, home from Leipzig in his jeans, and evinces a vague superiority to his present surroundings. In Munich, the opening ceremony is under way. Phalanxes of athletes jog forward on the track with huge flags. There is much talk of forgiveness, of progress, of peace — of how this is *not* 1936 — and a flock of white doves is unnetted into the stadium sky.

'And was there much excitement in the DDR about the Games?' Spiridon is still putting slightly obsequious questions to Aleksandr Ivanovich.

'No. Not at all,' he says. 'They're not happy about it, actually. I think they're hoping something bad's going to happen.' Spiridon looks shocked. 'Like what?' he says. Aleksandr Ivanovich says, 'I don't know,' and moves off to look for someone more interesting. Watching his nephew now, Aleksandr thinks of the first time that he saw him, of the night twenty-four years earlier when he fumbled open the front door in the small hours to see a lad of about twelve standing there with the nightwatchman from downstairs. 'Your brother's wife's having the baby,' he said. He was from one of the other families who lived in Ivan's flat — small, round-skulled, his head shaved. Sergey was his name. He looked very pale. They all did in the white incandescence of the nightwatchman's hissing kerosene lamp.

'Is everything alright?' Aleksandr said.

'I suppose so.'

'When did it start?'

Sergey just shrugged.

'Wait here. I'll come back with you.'

Zalesky's mother was standing in the hall. 'What is it?' she whispered.

'Nothing. Don't worry.'

Still asleep, Irina mumbled the same question. 'It's started,' he said. 'I'm going over there. Do you want to come?'

'Mn.'

For a few seconds she did not move and he said, 'You'd better hurry up — one of the kids from Vanya's place is waiting for us.'

She tutted, and sighed, and he heard her

slowly sit up. 'You'd better hurry up,' he said. She said nothing. 'You'd better . . . '

'I know!' She pulled her nightdress over her head; there were pink imprints on her skin where she had slept on its folds. She was trying to smoke and dress at the same time — with a cigarette in her mouth she was fastening her brassiere; then she transferred it quickly from one hand to the other as she put her arms through the short sleeves of her shirt. She left it in the ashtray for a few seconds while she put her skirt on.

'Alright?'

She nodded, pulling her shoes over her heels with a hooked finger.

He spent that night sitting on the floor in the stuffy hall of Ivan's flat, perspiring and sleepy. He thinks of the loud shuddering noises he heard from Ivan's room, and of how it seemed incredible to him that it was Katya making them. There was no trace of her normal voice in them. They did not even sound human. They were more like the violent protestations of a ship's timbers. He was woken from a light sleep by a short, tremulous waul, and thought involuntarily of Lear's words — '*When we are born, we cry that we are come to this great stage of fools* . . . ' Though the windowless hall was dark, under the doors were sharp lines of daylight. There was another waul. Then a peculiar quiet. Then voices talking. He could not hear what they were saying. He was very thirsty. Some time later — it might have been as much as an hour, he might have slept some more — Ivan suddenly opened the door. He looked more worried, more harassed, than he had until then. In the sunlight that poured into the hall through the open door Aleksandr saw how tired he was. 'Come in Sasha,' he said, without smiling. Squinting, he went into the room. Katya looked surprisingly well, though pale, some of her hair still stuck to her fore- hand. The windows were all wide open . . .

He thinks of the walk home, the sun hot, the trams full. He was worried that he had offended Ivan, that he had not seemed pleased — or not enough — when Katya told him they were naming their son after him. 'What should we do?' It was the first thing Irina had said since they left Ivan's flat. They were on the Plotinka. He laughed. A tired, sour laugh. 'I need to sleep,' he said, and a second later saw that she was no longer walking next to him. She had stopped. 'Irina . . . ' She shook her head. The heat of the sun was sweatily unpleasant. The shine of the water, even of the cobbled street, hurt his eyes. She started to walk away. He tried to take hold of her arm, and she immediately pulled it free and stepped out into the street. He overtook her at the foot of the steps on the other side of the dam, where the water tumbling through the sluice-gates was very loud. 'Is it because I said I need to sleep?' he shouted. 'I'm tired. I don't want to do anything. What do you want to do? Aren't you tired? I have to sleep.' He was standing in front of her, with the sun in his eyes . . .

And he thinks of how she entered their room, some hours later. He was sitting at the table, vacant with exhaustion, waiting for her. He had only slept for two hours, and when he woke she was still not there. He heard the front door of the flat open and shut. Then Irina's voice — sounding fine, vivacious — and the strong, hoarse voice of Zalesky's mother. He was not able to hear what they were saying. There was some laughter. Then Irina entered their room. Without saying a word, she shut the door, and lay face down on the divan. For a minute, feeling wretched, he watched her. Then he stood up and sat down next to her on the divan. 'What is it?' he said, putting his hand on her hip. 'Irishka, what is it?' She said nothing. And, of course, he knew what it was.

For Aleksandr Ivanovich, he thinks, that night, that morning — of which he has such vivid, living memories — are merely part of the hinterland that precedes memory. A hinterland mapped out in old photographs, of people he knows, not as he knows them. Young-faced. Playing other parts. A half-familiar setting, missing its most important element. Once, he pointed to a picture of Irina and said, 'Who's that?'

12

I did not expect her to telephone me, and soon stopped even hoping that she would, so I was surprised when one morning, perhaps two weeks later — it was the week that Zhdanov died — I picked up the phone and it was her. She said she was phoning from the lobby of the Iset hotel and wanted to see me. I walked over from the MGB offices, and found her waiting in the sunshine outside the hotel. A symbol of Sverdlovsk's postwar status, it towered over the wooden houses in the traditional Urals style that then lined Lenin Prospekt.

She had sounded nervous on the phone, and was nervous when we met. She did not know what to expect of me, I suppose. And what did I expect, as I walked over to the Iset that morning? I had her journal with me, and also some photographs that were found in her house. I took her to lunch in the hotel. The journal was a thick blue volume, a sort of heavy exercise book. On the front she had written 'Nadezhda Filippovna Podlubnaya, 1932'. It was tied shut with a strip of blue satin. She took the photographs. However, she said she did not want the journal. 'Are you sure?' I said.

'Yes. Do what you want with it. Throw it away.' She said this without vehemence, almost placidly, with a sort of smile.

'Throw it away?'

'Have you looked at it?'

'No.'

For a moment, only for a moment, she looked into my face, trying to see whether I was telling the truth. I think she thought I was lying. (Though I was not — I had not looked at it. Not then.) Perhaps that's why she said, 'I don't want it. Throw it away.'

'Okay. If that's what you want . . . '

'It's what I want. I'm ashamed of it.'

'Why?'

'I just am.' She smiled. Then she said she was sorry to trouble me, but she had arrived in town that morning and had nowhere to stay. I had said I might be able to help.

It was no small thing, in 1948, to find living space in Sverdlovsk. The population had doubled in only a few years. To my knowledge, there was only one immediate source of empty space — and, of course, we were not supposed to use it. Still — and I write this with some shame — I looked through the list, and found a professor of plant sciences at the Urals State Technical University — Yakov Shtern was his name — who had lived in a few square metres on Karl Libknekht Street. I went to see the place on my own, and found some of the neighbours in the process of moving in. 'What are you doing?' I said. 'Who are you? This room was supposed to be sealed.' I shooed them off and went in myself. It was quite spacious, and had obviously been vacated in a hurry. The bed was unmade. Things were scattered on the floor. The shelves had been thoroughly searched. There was a stale, unpleasant odour emanating from the leftovers of a meal, now mouldy, on the table. I opened the single large window, which overlooked the street, and let in some fresh air. I threw out the mouldy leftovers. I tidied up.

The next morning I showed it to her. 'Whose room is it?' she said. When I told her, she seemed surprised, though I don't know how else she thought I would find something. She asked how long she would be able to stay there. 'I don't know,' I said.

Over the next few weeks, the last weeks of summer, I went to see her sometimes. She knew no-one in Sverdlovsk. No-one who would see her anyway. Sometimes I took her to lunch at the Ural restaurant, which had opened since the war and was nearby. She had very little money, and had left Metelyev Log with only one small suitcase, so I bought her some new clothes at the Ministry of State Security store, and a pair of shoes, as well as soap and some other necessities. Once or twice, I took her to the Turkish baths — there was no hot water in Shtern's flat — and signed her in to the First Department.

★ ★ ★

It was in those weeks too, the last weeks of summer, that my final meeting with her husband took place in my office one evening. 'Some tea and sandwiches, please,' I said to Voronin, when he ushered him in. 'Oh, and some cigarettes.' Then I sat down. Not at my desk, on the straight-backed seat usually used by visitors, and indicated to Lozovsky to take the chaise longue. 'Please.' He hesitated for a moment. He looked tired and had lost weight. His shoes had no laces.

'This isn't a formal interview,' I said. 'As you see there's no stenographer. No witnesses. There'll be no record of what we say. I just wanted to talk to you. And if you want to ask me anything, feel free.'

'Has my wife been arrested?' he said immediately.

'No. Why would she be?'

'I don't know. But then I don't know why I was. And I don't expect you'll tell me.'

131

'I will,' I said.

Voronin wheeled in the tea and sandwiches. The first thing Lozovsky wanted, however, was a cigarette. Unfortunately I didn't have any matches, and had to ask Voronin to light it for him. 'Leave the matches,' I said. I passed Lozovsky an ashtray and for a minute or two he smoked in silence. Then he had some tea. 'Am I allowed to know what happened to Yudin?' he said.

'I don't see why not. He was brought to Sverdlovsk. A ministry doctor had a look at him.'

'And?'

'And he's been sent home.'

'Home?'

'To live with his mother. She lives in a settlement near here. You shouldn't have been so stubborn. You should have signed the form.' He stared at me for what seemed like a long time. I shrugged. 'Well, it's made no difference,' I said. 'Except for you.' As soon as I had said this I saw the implication of it, and that he had seen it too. He opened his mouth to speak. Then he saw that I knew what he was going to say, and this seemed to satisfy him. 'May I?' He indicated the sandwiches.

'Of course. They're for you.'

He wolfed down one or two sandwiches very quickly. He must have been hungry, but in fact he always ate like that. I had noticed it at Metelyev Log.

I leaned over and switched on the light on my desk. 'I've been wanting to ask you,' I said. 'Why did you leave the Second Medical Institute and take the job at Metelyev Log? It was a significant step down.'

'That was years ago,' he said, with his mouth full.

'I know.'

He seemed to have nothing more to say on the subject, so while he finished eating, I said, 'They're going to close Metelyev Log, you know, and transfer the patients to Kisegach.'

'Are they?'

'Yes. Your work was the only thing that justified keeping it open — '

'You said you'd tell me why I was arrested.'

I did not like the way he interrupted me. I was trying to be friendly, though now my voice probably lost some of its friendliness. 'There was something you wrote in the thirties,' I said. 'A piece for a scientific journal. In 1936. I'm sure you know the piece I'm talking about. In it you speculated that the sense of order we have about the world is essentially subjective, is simply a product of our minds. We talked about these things when I was at Metelyev Log. There was a fuss at the time — it turned political — you had influential friends who

133

protected you. Well, now someone's found it, and they want to talk to you about it. I presume that's what's happened. I don't know for sure.' Having finished the sandwiches, he lit a cigarette. 'Of course, you wrote it twelve years ago. Your ideas might have moved on since then.' My tone was questioning. 'Have they? As I said, this is entirely informal. Whatever you say will stay in this room. You have my word on that. I'm just interested.'

'Your word?' he said.

I now think that this was probably sarcastic. Then, I took it as a sincere question and said, 'Yes.'

'The piece you're talking about was a scientific paper.'

'Yes.'

'Its subject was neuropsychology. Politics had nothing to do with it.'

'Well . . .' I smiled. 'Politics has to do with everything. Neither of us is in a position to say what is political and what isn't. No one is. And no one can escape from politics. Not you. Not me. Except perhaps through total solitude. Robinson Crusoe. Until man Friday turns up — then you have politics.' I was uneasily aware of trying to impress him. 'You must be able to see how what you wrote in that paper might turn into a political issue?'

'It was turned into a political issue by other

people. It's got nothing to do with me. My work was pure science.'

'Even if the things they said followed logically, even inevitably, from your ideas?'

'What things? What did they say? I don't know.'

'Taking your ideas as a starting point, they said, in so many words, that there's no such thing as truth, that life is inherently meaningless, history just a meaningless struggle of all against all. A sort of nihilism, in other words. Or at least an extreme form of scepticism, which is in effect the same thing. Is that what you think too? I'm just interested. You can speak honestly to me.' When he did not, I smiled and said, 'Well, I think it is what you think.'

He laughed. 'Why?'

I opened one of my desk drawers. 'Do you know this book?' I said, taking it out and holding it up for a moment. His face showed nothing, or only the slightest tightening of the jaw. 'I found it in your office at Metelyev Log. It was the only book there, as far as I could see, that wasn't a medical text book. It's a book about music. About Johann Sebastian Bach in particular.' He stared at me impassively. 'You like puzzles, don't you?' I said. 'Logic puzzles, word puzzles? This book involves a word puzzle — a hidden one. It's to do with the name of the author. Nikolay Maksimovich Luzhov. The strange thing is, this Nikolay Maksimovich Luzhov doesn't seem to exist. Did you know that? I've looked into it.'

'I don't know anything about him.'

'And his book was published only two years ago. Then it occurred to me where, exactly, I found it. Where in your office. On which shelf. It was on the shelf with your books — I mean, with books written by you. Of course, it might have found its way there by mistake. That's what I thought at first. And then,' I said, 'then I noticed — and this is where the word puzzle comes in — I noticed something about the name Nikolay Maksimovich Luzhov. It's an anagram. An anagram of another name. Your name.'

When he did not deny that he had written the little volume — and I think part of him was pleased, even under the circumstances, that someone had solved his puzzle; the pseudonym, after all, did not have to be an anagram of his own name — I opened it and looked for the first passage that I had marked.

'You start,' I said, 'with a quotation from someone — Schweitzer is his name — writing about Johann Sebastian Bach. 'He inscribed the work completed in Cöthen the 'Well-tempered Clavier' by way of celebrating a victory that gave the musical world of that day a satisfaction which we can easily comprehend. On the old keyed instruments it had become impossible to play in all the keys, since the fifths and thirds were tuned naturally, according to the absolute intervals given by the divisions of the string. By this method each separate key was made quite true; the others, however, were more or less out of tune, the thirds and fifths that were right for one key not being right for another. So a method had to be found for tuning fifths and thirds not absolutely but relatively, — to 'temper' them in such a way that though not quite true in any one key they would be bearable in all. The question occupied the attention of the Italians Gioseffo Zarlino (1558) and Pietro Aron (1529). At a later date the Halberstadt organ builder Andreas Werckmeister (1645–1706) hit upon the method of tuning that still holds today. He divided the octave into twelve equal semitones, none of which was quite true. His treatise 'Musical Temperament' appeared in 1691. The problem was solved; henceforth composers could write in all the keys. A fairly long time elapsed, however, before all the keys hitherto avoided came into practical use. The celebrated theoretician Heinichen, in his treatise on the thorough-bass, published in 1728, — i.e. six years after the origin of Bach's work — confessed that people seldom wrote in B major and A flat major, and practically never in F sharp minor and C sharp minor; which shows that he did not know Bach's collection of preludes and fugues.' You then spend the next two hundred pages,' I said, 'taking issue with various points in Schweitzer's text. Your main point is that the phrase 'the problem was solved' suggests a problem, and a solution, understood in empirical terms. In fact, you say, in the early eighteenth century many methods of tuning existed, of which equal temperament was only one, and one which was in no way seen as being empirically or self-evidently superior to the others. You say that it had existed in various forms since about 1675, and was only taken up universally in the mid eighteenth century. In the intervening period there was a violent difference of opinion as to whether it was an improvement, or in fact an impoverishment, of the pre-existing situation. Even Werckmeister himself, the man who Schweitzer tells us invented the method of equal temperament, did not personally favour it until a theologian persuaded him that its proportions somehow matched those of Solomon's palace as set out in the Bible — from our point of view, as you say, something entirely nonsensical. Until then, he preferred another method, the so-called 'Werckmeister III', which did not involve equal temperament

— and which was quite possibly the method favoured by Bach himself. So the term 'well-tempered' in Bach's title does not even necessarily mean 'equally tempered', and might just as easily refer to 'Werckmeister III', or some other method of tuning. Many people at the time thought equal temperament sounded 'wrong', and Bach may have been one of them. That it does not sound 'wrong' to us, you say, just shows how subjective these things are, and how wrong we are to think of the equal-temperament scale as 'some sort of fundamental musical material'. That we do think of it in those terms is simply because of the sort of music that has been written for the last two hundred years — music for which it is indeed a fundamental material. You insist that none of this should lessen our esteem for Bach and his work. In fact, you say that its position as the foundation of modern European tonality is even more impressive when we understand that this was not inevitable — that it won that status for itself, that it made something ex nihilo, and did not simply stumble on something that somehow pre-existed and was just waiting to be found. And you end with a second quotation from Schweitzer, which I liked very much. 'Nevertheless, overwhelmed as we are by the intellectual and organisational achievements of this work, we must not lose sight of the fact that they would mean little were it not for the profound and humane beauty of every one of the pieces contained therein. Joy, sorrow, tears, lamentation, laughter: to all of these it gives voice, but in such a way that we are transported from the world of restless imperfection to an ideal world of peace, and see reality in a new way: as it were, sitting by a mountain lake and contemplating hills and woods and clouds in the placid and fathomless water. Whoever has once felt this perfect serenity has comprehended the mysterious spirit that has here expressed all it knew in the language of tone, and will render Bach the thanks we render only to those great souls to whom it is given to reconcile men with life and bring them peace.' Is that a fair summary?'

'No,' Lozovsky said.

'No?'

'You make it sound like a polemical tract. It's not.'

'You don't think what I've said is a fair summary?'

'No, I don't. It's a technical work. It's about the tuning of musical instruments. Most of it's taken up with technical detail, which you haven't even mentioned.'

I looked at him for a few moments. 'I'll be honest with you,' I said. 'I see this as an

Aesopian work. I see it as a restatement of the ideas expressed in your 1936 paper. Only here the political implications are more obvious — if we take 'equal temperament' to stand for 'Marxism'. I smiled. 'Well? What do you say? I've been honest with you. That's what I think.'

'It's fanciful,' he said.

'Is it?'

'And even if it were true, which it isn't, the 'Well-tempered Clavier' would presumably stand for 1917, and Bach for Lenin, and I have only love and veneration for Bach and his work.'

'And for Lenin and his, I hope! No, it's true. What you say is true. The problem is more subtle. You may love and venerate Bach and his work, and you may even love and venerate Lenin and his — however, you see neither the equal-temperament scale nor Marxism as having an intrinsic progressive truth. Something else might do just as well. Neither is historically inevitable. Nothing is, in your view.'

'I don't know what makes you say that.'

'No? What about this. You write, 'Looking into the past, we are tempted to see the pre-tonal world of the seventeenth century as missing something essential, as existing in darkness, waiting for the tonal light — or at most as a series of primitive, painful steps towards the future of tonality as we know it, founded on the equal-temperament scale, as if this were somehow an end point towards which everything had been progressing from the start.' Isn't that a denial of the very idea of progress?'

For the first time he seemed to lose his self-possession slightly. 'Progress? I'm talking about music there. What would progress mean, in musical terms? Perhaps you'll tell me. I don't understand.'

'That's my point.'

'What's your point?'

'Do you believe that history moves forward in a meaningful way?' I said.

'History? Perhaps.'

'Perhaps?' There was an uneasy silence while I turned the pages of the book. 'You take exception to Schweitzer's use of the word 'victory', I said. ' 'He inscribed the work completed in Cöthen the 'Well-tempered Clavier' by way of celebrating a victory . . . ' It's the same point, essentially. Just another instance of the subjectivism which is the keynote of the whole thing.' I shut the book and smiled. 'You think I'm being silly, I know. It's not important. It's just my little theory. I'm not planning to send this book to Moscow, if that's what you're worried about. When you get there you'll be asked whether you still hold the views you expressed in your 1936 paper, and in the papers influenced by yours. You'll be

142

invited to disown those views. Which I don't think you will, since they are your views, and you're very proud and stubborn. And honest.' He said nothing. 'You understand, of course, that it's impossible for someone who holds such views to occupy a prominent position in our public life. Especially in an educational establishment. And what else would you do? Work on a farm? In a factory? You'll be sentenced to ten years. In a special prison, if you're willing to work in one. Life is not unpleasant in those places, especially for someone like you. I mean, someone who lives for their work.' I stood up and poured him some more tea from the little stainless-steel samovar on the trolley. He had been listening to what I said with a stony, expressionless face. Or perhaps he was not listening. He was not looking at me. 'On a personal level,' I said, 'I'm very sorry that this is the situation we find ourselves in. I'll never forget the week I spent at Metelyev Log, your kindness to me. I want to thank you for that.'

'What will happen to my wife?' he said.

'Your wife?'

'Yes.'

'I don't know. Nothing.'

'If you feel we were kind to you . . . ' For the first time in several minutes he looked me in the eye. He was more upset than he seemed. I felt very sorry for him.

'I'll try to help her,' I said.

'Thank you.'

'And thank you for talking to me.' I picked up the phone. He immediately lit another cigarette. 'Take them with you,' I said. 'And the matches.' He seemed to ignore this. While I was speaking to Voronin, however, he put them in his pocket.

That was the last time I saw him. Leaving the office that night, an hour or two later, I said to Voronin, 'Turn off his light, and make sure he has a proper pillow. He needs to sleep.' He was taken to Moscow the next morning.

★ ★ ★

Somewhere in our talk, I'm not sure where — and of course what I have just written is only from memory and a sort of stylisation of what took place — I said to Lozovsky that there was a sentence in his book that I had particularly liked. 'Where is it?' I said, leafing through the pages. 'It's when you're explaining the problems involved in tuning keyed instruments, which you explain very well, very lucidly. I found the whole book very interesting. You say that the problem is similar to that associated with leap years — that the smaller natural units do not fit exactly into the larger natural units — days into years, pure major thirds into octaves. And then you say, 'The difference is small, but the imperfection is total.' I liked that. 'The difference is small, but the imperfection is total.' '

★   ★   ★

It was in those weeks too, the last weeks of summer, that your second piece on him was published, Ivan. Much talk of 'Cosmopolitan scum'. One morning I looked at the newspaper, and on the front page there was a picture of Lozovsky. His eyes were in shadow. He looked evil, monstrous. I don't know exactly how you ended up writing the piece illustrated by that photograph. Only you know that. His wife saw it. She said, 'What's happened to Misha? Where is he?' I said I didn't know. Probably in Moscow. And she said, 'I know he's done something terrible, but I feel so sorry for him.' It was the only time I saw her cry, standing in the window light, with her hands over her face. And then it was reprinted in 'Pravda'! On the front page! Your name prominent! I intended to speak to you about it. I was upset and went over what I would say to you many times in my mind. I wanted to make sure that you, at least, understood that whatever else he might be — and he was not innocent — he was not the monster depicted in your text. In the end, I never did speak to you about it. Or not until the night we lost to West Germany in the football, when I tried to, and you said you had forgotten.

I think your piece influenced his fate. I thought, until I saw it, that he would be sent to a special prison, to pursue his work in well-fed obscurity, in a mansion surrounded by slash-wire in some Moscow suburb. Probably that did not seem punishment enough for 'Cosmopolitan scum'. He went to a lumber camp in the Far East, and there, in the swamp and forest of a nameless river system, he died. That was in 1951.

Now let's turn to 1960, and what happened then. He was posthumously judged to have been totally innocent. The judgement was issued by Khrushchev's Supreme Court, and widely published in the newspapers. And that meant trouble for us, Ivan — for you and me. Your name was still proudly on the front page of that old edition of 'Pravda', there was no escaping that unfortunate fact. And I was the officer who had put together the original prosecution materials in forty-eight. No escaping that either. So what did we have to say for ourselves?

I was frightened, Ivan. I was very frightened. As you know, some people in my position were shot. That was not out of the question. The new men, Khrushchev's men, were in power. They looked very sober as they sat in judgement on me, but I knew they were smirking inside to see me squirm. So what did I say? I said that I did not think Lozovsky was innocent. I said I thought he had held and hoped to propagate views that were profoundly inimical to the making of Communism. I said that I did not think the verdict should have been overturned. Somehow, from somewhere — perhaps from a lingering shame that I had not fought in the war — I found the strength to say those things.

I know you were frightened too, Ivan — though no journalists were being shot. You might have lost your job though. You might have been publicly vilified. So under the eyes of your judges and your peers, you said what they wanted you to say. With your hand shaking, you said the lines they had written for you — 'What I did was wrong. And I knew it was wrong. And I'm sorry.'

What I want to know — what I have always wanted to know — is whether you meant it. Did you mean it when you said, 'What I did was wrong. And I knew it was wrong. And I'm sorry.' If you meant it, if you thought it was wrong when you did it — well, that's a terrible thing to own up to, and a terrible thing to have done. And if you did not think it was wrong when you did it, then you were a liar and a hypocrite to say, twelve years later, that you did.

Perhaps, though, you don't know yourself what you thought. Perhaps you did not know even at the time. In 1948 and then in 1960, you did not know whether what you were doing was wrong or not — you simply took your lead from those around you, from what they seemed to think, from what they seemed to want.

I don't know why I wasn't shot. I suspect because even in Khrushchev's time there were people in positions of power who understood and sympathised with what I had done, and silently intervened to save me. So I was a KGB colonel for twelve more years. There was no work for me though. For the past twelve years I have done nothing. I don't know if you knew that. You must have suspected it. And then, in February, the quiet event in the officers' mess. Hushed-up, a poor turnout, no one senior there. I was presented with that watch you tell me I should wear, the Vostok or whatever it is, with the service insignia, the sword and shield, on its black face. And that was that.

And you? Since your performance in front of the judges you have prospered. True, there were a few years in the early sixties when you had a hunted look. You were moved from news to sport. That was a step down, of course — though you did a lot of travelling, which you seemed to like. You were moved back to news in sixty-four — I remember that New Year's Eve party: you were jubilant, laughing and throwing snowballs like an excited teenager. Did you feel that you had been forgiven? What you have to understand is there is no forgiveness — that's the stuff of Christianity. Our failings are unforgivable. We have to live with them forever. That is, until we die.

13

Something has happened in Munich. On the radio they say there has been 'an incident' which has led to the suspension of the Olympic Games. In Sverdlovsk it is early evening. He switches on the electric light in the kitchen, opens the mesh-fronted larder and takes out the simple elements of his evening meal. The Olympics have been satisfactory so far — in spite of the Jew Spitz's seven world records in a week. His participation in proceedings was particularly infuriating on Monday when the United States won the men's four-hundred-metre freestyle relay — with Spitz swimming the final leg, overtaking Grivennikov and forcing the Soviet team into the silver medal position. And something similar happened in the eight-hundred-metre event on Thursday — only there the Soviet Union did not even hold on for silver, which, sickeningly, went to West Germany. Earlier the same day, however, Aleksandr Medved had taken on the American Chris Taylor — a no-neck one-hundred-and-eighty-kilo monster — in the super-heavyweight wrestling, and somehow

150

emerged victorious; and on Friday Valery Borzov triumphed on the track in the hundred metres. The USSR mopped up most of the medals in the women's gymnastics; the men's team, unfortunately, losing out to the nimble Japanese. And in the final of the eight hundred metres on Saturday, Yevgeni Arzhanov seemed certain to win only to 'hit the wall' near the finish, presenting first place to Dave Wottle — of the USA, naturally — and literally falling over the line. Nevertheless, the medals table now has a familiar look to it.

He is wondering what the 'incident' might be which has led to the suspension when his thoughts are unexpectedly interrupted by the sound of the doorbell. With his mouth full, he looks out of the living-room window and sees Ivan's plum-black Lada parked in the autumn twilight.

He lets him in and leads him up the stairs. Ivan is very short-winded. This does not stop him lighting a cigarette.

'Are you alright?' Aleksandr says.

'Yes, I'm fine. Well . . . something's happened.'

'Sit down.'

Ivan flops onto the sofa. 'Can I have . . . some water, please?' When he has had some water, he says, 'Have you heard they've suspended the Olympic Games?'

'Yes, of course. Why? What's happened?'

'What are they saying? On the radio.'

'Nothing. They say there's been an 'incident'. What's happened?'

'Palestinian terrorists have taken fifteen Israeli athletes hostage,' Ivan says. 'They've already killed two of them. It's been going on since this morning. They're demanding the release of prisoners held in Israel.'

'They've already killed two of them?'

'They were threatening to kill them all at noon, then they said they'd kill one every hour until the prisoners were released. But the Israelis refused point blank to release them. Then the Germans got the deadline extended to five o'clock.' He looks at his watch. 'So nine o'clock here. In a couple of hours. I have to go back and see what happens. At the moment, we've been told not to report it. Not to talk about it. I'm going to be up all night — that's obvious.'

'You look tired,' Aleksandr says.

'I am tired. This all started this morning. And Kaminsky's on holiday in Egypt. They can't even get him on the phone.' Oleg Kaminsky, managing editor of the *Urals Worker*. 'I have to go back soon.'

'Do you want some tea?'

'Yes. Please.'

'The Germans are going out of their

minds,' he says, when the tea is made. 'They can't believe this is happening. Some German politician even offered his own life in place of the Israelis'. It's a nightmare for them. And an embarrassment for us. That's why we're not saying anything yet. They want to see how it ends before they decide what to say. What they *want* to say is: 'Look how desperate the poor Palestinians are. If they weren't so oppressed they wouldn't be doing this.' And that's what we will say, when it's over, if it ends without a massacre. At the moment it's all too ugly though. They threw the body of one of the dead athletes over a balcony. If it ends in a massacre you won't hear about it. It won't be political anyway. We're supposed to portray the Palestinians as victims, not murderers.'

'They are victims.'

'They don't look like victims today. I've seen the German TV pictures. The main terrorist is a weird-looking guy in a white suit and a white panama hat with black shoe polish on his face and a grenade in his hand at all times. The Germans are saying they're from some fanatical extreme fringe group of the PLO. There's just such a sense of shock. *I'm* in shock. The pictures are surreal. There's people just going on with things in the Olympic village — sunbathing, playing table tennis, training.' He shakes his head and lights a Golden Fleece. 'The IOC didn't want to suspend but there was such outrage that they had to. That was the last thing I heard. I'm not supposed to be talking about it.'

'I won't tell anyone.'

'I know. I'd better get back.' He stands up, and for a moment seems to sway unsteadily. He even puts out a hand, which Aleksandr seizes.

'Are you sure you're alright, Vanya?'

'I'm tired, that's all. And I haven't eaten all day.'

'Do you want something?'

'No, thanks. I'm not hungry.'

'Are you sure?'

'Thanks.'

He leaves, and a minute later Aleksandr hears the Lada start, and stall, and start, and drive away.

★ ★ ★

In the morning he walks to the news-stand. The radio had nothing more to say on the subject of the Olympic suspension the previous night; however the headline in the *Urals Worker* is 'OLYMPIC HOSTAGES FREED'. He starts on the story as he walks home, walking slowly with his eyes on the newsprint. It says

154

that the terrorists wanted a long-range jet to take them and the hostages to an unspecified Arab country. The Germans said they would provide one and flew them to the airport in helicopters. It was a trap and there was a firefight on the airport tarmac in which all the terrorists were killed and all the hostages freed. There is also a prominent op-ed piece — judging by the style, he thinks Ivan might have penned it himself — on the oppression that led the Palestinians to use such extreme means to make their plight known to the world.

It is a windy, overcast, September morning. Turning into Studencheskaya Street, he looks up from the paper. Ivan's Lada is parked outside the flat — he has just tried the doorbell and is standing next to the tarnished-silver trunk of the cherry tree looking up at the first-floor windows. Then, seeing Aleksandr, he starts to walk towards him. It is obvious that he has not slept all night; he looks even more tired and puffy than he did yesterday. The pouches under his eyes are black and painful-looking. 'Forget it,' he says. 'It's rubbish.'

'What is?'

'What it says in the newspaper.'

'What do you mean?'

'They're all dead.'

'Who are?'

'The hostages. They're all dead.'

Aleksandr unlocks the door and they step into the damp hall.

'Then why say they were all freed?' he says quietly. 'That's a stupid lie . . . '

'It wasn't a lie,' Ivan says. 'It was a mistake.' He looks terrible, ill. 'The Germans announced that they had freed all the hostages and killed all the terrorists. That was at about 2 a.m. here, and we were told to go with it. Put it on the front page. Then two hours later an IOC spokesman said the first statement may have been 'too optimistic'. Then they said everyone was dead. There was a firefight at the airport that went on for hours. It was a farce. In the end the terrorists just blew themselves and the hostages up. And we'd already printed *that*,' he says. 'They wouldn't wait. They'd heard what they wanted to hear and they told us to print it. And now I'm the one who looks like I've fucked up.' He has tears in his eyes. 'I'm sick of it, Sasha,' he says.

'Sick of what?'

'I don't know. I'm just worn out. I'm sorry. It's been a terrible night.'

'You need to sleep.'

'Yes. Yes, I know.' He lights a Golden Fleece and sighs exhaustedly. 'Did I tell you about the leader of the terrorists,' he says, 'the one who wore a panama hat and had black shoe polish on his face?'

'Yes.'

'He was an extraordinary character. I saw the German TV pictures. He'd just spoiled the Olympic Games, he was totally surrounded, unlikely to survive, and he seemed so sure of himself, of what he was doing. It was extraordinary! And you know what I thought?' Ivan laughs. 'I thought, I should try to be more like him! Less emotional about everything. Less worried about what people will think of me.'

'He was a fanatic.'

'I worry too much, I know.'

'You should go home and sleep, Vanya.'

'They won't make me editor now.'

'It wasn't your fault.'

'Oh, they'll make sure it was.' Though he looks utterly miserable, he laughs. He never hides his feelings, his failures. Even when he tries, he is unable to. It is why people love him, in spite of everything. The very figure of a mature and worldly male, handsome and well dressed, he looks lost and tearful in his moment of failure. Standing there in the stone-floored hall, Aleksandr is unexpectedly filled with love for him. He smiles. 'Never mind,' he says, and still holding the newspaper, he embraces him. 'You need some sleep, Vanya,' he says, with his hands on his sleeves. 'You need some sleep.'

When Ivan has left, Aleksandr walks slowly up the stairs, listening to the persistent yur-yurring of the Lada. He throws the newspaper onto the sofa and sits down. He sits there for a long time, in front of his typewriter — an old machine which he salvaged from the office when the KGB invested in new electric ones in the late sixties. On most of its keys the white letter has been typed into an illegible scatter of specks. On some of them — А, Е, И, О, У, С, Ш — even into nothing, leaving the smooth tablet unmarked. He spools a new sheet of off-white paper onto the cylinder. His thoughts have turned from the events of the summer of 1948 to those of the autumn.

He does not know where to start. Where indeed? In a sense the starting point would be all the way back in the spring, the night he returned from Metelyev Log for the first time. It was late, the electricity was off, and Irina was asleep. Stepping through the darkness, he kicked something — it sounded like a glass with a spoon in it. There was a sharp, furious *shh!* from the divan. 'Sorry,' he whispered, and there was another, softer *shh*, and she turned on the tired springs. He knew then that he had a secret. It was no more than an innocent little infatuation, nurtured on afternoons spent sitting at the table in the wooden house, the rain falling into the forest that started immediately outside the windows, the wood hissing and whining in the stove. Still, it was a secret, and the feeling of isolation took him by surprise as soon as he was in Irina's sleeping presence. He undressed and slipped under the sheet, next to her warm weight, touching her warm legs and feet with his own. Sleepily she turned over to face him. For the next two months Nadezhda Lozovskaya did not seem part of the world they lived in — the world of Malyshev Street, and Lenin Prospekt, the MGB offices, and the thinly stocked shoe-shop where Irina worked. She was like a figment of his imagination. She *was* a figment of his imagination, whom he had no expectation of ever meeting under the spacious sky, in the wide streets of Sverdlovsk. He hardly noticed at first (to use a Sputnik-era metaphor) the mysterious pull on his settled orbit exerted by this seemingly weightless figment of his imagination — and its influence on his life was then more or less imperceptible, in effect no more than a sense of possibility.

He was innocently uxorious; he was the sort of man of whom it was said that he 'never even looked at another woman'; his love for his wife, in the spring of 1948, was plain and natural — that is, it seemed plain and natural to him, when he thought about it at all. They had been married since 1934 — had lived since 1937 in the flat on Malyshev Street which they shared with Major Ivan Ivanovich Zalesky, and his wife and mother. Zalesky — to whom their room was 'the ballroom', with its peeling gilt moulding and vestigial chandelier — intermittently schemed to swap it for one of the two slightly smaller spaces in which he and his increasingly numerous family lived. He said they didn't need all that parquet. *They* did not have an increasingly numerous family. They did not have a family at all. Irina had had two miscarriages in the mid-thirties — the second time having to deliver a dead thing, a dead son — and the experiences had left their mark on her. On him too, and on their life together. Most of all on her though. Her eyes, the lines of her mouth. She was not the same after that. She started to smoke herself to sleep in the mid-afternoon. He spent more time at work. The subject was not spoken of anymore. It was their sad secret.

14

The day you got home from work early. It was
September. Your hair was wet. Rain-sodden
ringlets. 'What is it?' I said. I had been
sleeping. I was working nights that week. 'Why
are you home so early? What's happened?' You
started to wrench open drawers, and search
violently through them. 'What is it?'

'I've been sacked,' you said, tipping a
drawerful of stuff onto the floor.

'What are you doing?'

You tipped out another drawer.

'Stop it! What are you looking for? What's
going on? Why were you sacked?'

You said you had had a brooch on the lapel
of your coat when you went to work. At
lunchtime it wasn't there, and you had accused
Svidersky's wife of stealing it. Sviderskaya, of
course, had instantly lost her temper. I was
able to picture the scene. Pushing imperiously
past you, she would have started shouting,
'Miron! Miron!' Her voice, when she told
Svidersky what had happened, would have
been quiet with fury. 'How can you stand for
this?' she would have said. 'How can you stand
for this?' Perhaps the second time her voice

161

would have soared to a shriek, especially if you were standing there in tears. And Miron — old Miron Svidersky — would have shoved his whiskers into his weskit and shaken his head. He would have sighed.

You said that Sviderskaya had stolen things from you in the past, that things had vanished from the pockets of your coat. You said that she hated you, that she was jealous of you. That was what you said.

Her voice screaming in the stock room would have been audible to the women queuing in the shop, steaming in their oilskin coats. (And there were many more of them queuing outside, as I saw myself when I went there later. A shipment of shoes had arrived that morning, and word had spread through the city.) 'She never does any work! What does she get paid for? Why is she here?' I knew the sort of thing Sviderskaya would have said, and I imagined Miron saying, 'Sh, sh . . . Quiet.' And Sviderskaya screaming 'No!' and storming out. And Miron lighting a papirosa in the stunned stock room — he would have offered you one, if you were still there, and lit it for you. The two of you would have smoked in silence for a few minutes. Then he would have said, 'Irishka, this isn't easy for me. And it's not just about this. Today. It's not just about today . . . '

You were still sifting through the stuff on

the floor. When you found it — it was nothing more than a piece of painted glass with a safety pin pasted to it — you wiped your eyes.

'You found it?' I said, noticing the sudden stillness.

'M-hm.'

'Do you want me to speak to Miron?'

'I don't know.' You were taking a cigarette from the pocket of your coat. Only when you were lying on the divan did you light it. The ashtray — a seashell — was on the parquet near your head. Half a cigarette was enough to send you to sleep. You let it slip from your fingers and turned your face to the wall. Such was your habit — to smoke half a cigarette and knock yourself out in the middle of the afternoon. An obvious symptom of unhappiness. I felt sad and helpless. I felt so helpless, Irishka. That sleep was like an immovable object. It was stubborn, sullen. Sometimes I was angry. Your slack face open-mouthed in the daylight — it was the only time you ever looked ugly to me — seemed like an indictment. And in a way it was, for my failure to make you happy. I did not know what I should do though. 'Why are you sleeping?' I would sometimes shout in this mood, when I took it so personally. When I tried to wake you, you shoved me away.

I went to the shop. The queue of women

spilled out onto the street. Some of them held newspapers over their heads to protect themselves from the rain. Inside, I pushed my way to the front — some of the women tried to stop me, until they saw my uniform (I had put it on specially) — where Miron was politely shouting, 'One pair each, ladies! Only one pair each!' When he saw me emerge from the wall of frantic women he frowned for a moment. Then he looked at me with a strained smile, and said, 'Aleksandr Andreyevich . . . ?' We withdrew into the stock room, leaving the shop-girls to put shoes into thrusting hands. Towering over her husband, Sviderskaya did not try to hide her feelings. With her arms folded and her cardigan on her shoulders like a shawl, she stared at me furiously. I said that you were not sleeping well, that you had made a mistake, that you were very sorry, and that it would mean a lot to me, personally, if he would let you keep your job.

He sighed.

'Miron!' Sviderskaya snapped.

He shrugged weakly. 'Okay,' he said, shaking his head. 'I'll take her back.'

'Thank you.'

Sviderskaya left, slamming the door. Miron lowered his head. I knew that his wife stole from the stock, and he knew that I knew.

Unfortunately that was not the end of it. As

we know, it was only the start. Sviderskaya had a niece who was a waitress at the Ural restaurant. This niece had once met me and had told Sviderskaya that she had seen me there with a woman. So perhaps a week later, when you had kissed and made up, Sviderskaya took you to one side in the stock room and told you sadly over a papirosa that your husband was seeing someone else. He often took her to lunch — this tall, elegant woman he was seeing — at the Ural restaurant. 'My niece is one of the waitresses there. She's seen them. She's even served them . . . '

'Do you go to the Ural restaurant?' you said to me that night.

It was obvious that this was not just an ordinary question, though you tried to make it sound like one. Something had upset you — I saw that immediately — and when you mentioned the Ural I knew what it was.

'Yes,' I said. 'Sometimes. Why?'

'I was speaking to Sviderskaya today.'

'Oh yes? What did she say?'

'She said you take a woman there.'

'Did she?'

'Is it true?'

'Yes.'

You looked as though someone had slapped you. Tears of shock. 'Who?'

'How does Sviderskaya know?' I said.

'Who IS she?'

I told you that she was the wife of a friend of mine who was in hospital. I said this because I did not want Sviderskaya to know that she was the wife of a prisoner, a political, someone vilified in the press. I said I had promised my friend that I would look out for his wife while he was ill. 'Don't you understand?' I said. 'Sviderskaya's just trying to upset you. Once or twice I've taken her to lunch. I've lent her some money. That's it.'

'Who is he? Who is this 'friend'?'

'You don't know him.'

'Why not?'

'You just don't.'

'What's wrong with him?'

Seeing that there would be no end to your questions, and not wanting to tell you more lies, I told you the truth. 'He's not in hospital,' I said. 'He's in prison.'

'In prison?'

'Yes.'

'Then why did you tell me he was in hospital?'

'I don't want Sviderskaya to know. You mustn't tell her . . . '

'Why didn't you tell me about her?'

'Who?'

'This woman!'

'Why would I? It's not important.'

'How old is she?' you said.
'How old is she?'
'Yes.'
'I don't know. Mid-thirties?' In fact she was thirty-one.
'What does she look like?'
'What?'
'What does she look like?'
'She's . . . quite tall. I don't know . . . What does it matter?'
'What's her name?'
'Her name?'
'Yes. What is it?'
To say the name felt like a transgression. Simply to say the name. Such was our innocence, Irinushka. You see, nothing had happened. If a handshake is something, then nothing had happened. That was what I tried to tell you. Faced with your suspicion I was filled with a fierce sense of my own innocence. And you were more and more suspicious. I stood next to a woman wearing perfume on the tram and you sniffed it on me. I had to work unexpectedly late one night and found you furious, in tears, packing a suitcase. The more I protested my innocence, the more you thought I was lying, the less you trusted me. Why did you not trust me? You opened my letters, went through my pockets. You found nothing of course. There was nothing to find.

Then you found something. Or you thought you did. You found 'Our Friends'. I had wondered whether to leave this novel — with its unfortunate inscription on the flyleaf: 'With warmest thanks, N' — in my office. In the end, I took it home. Why wouldn't I? I had nothing to hide.

Though I stuffed in into a shelf, you found it quickly. And you must have read it — you knew exactly what it was about. That too was unfortunate. The friendship, love affair, and finally marriage, of a young widow and a state security officer.

When I got home it was there on the table.

'Who's N?' you said.

'Who do you think?'

'Your mysterious Nadezhda?'

'Yes. She's not mine.'

'Isn't she?'

'No.'

'Well she seems quite taken with you.'

'Don't be silly.'

You snatched the novel from the table and started to read a passage aloud. You had obviously prepared this performance — selected the passage, marked it with a piece of paper. It was a love scene, somewhat trite. 'Stop it,' I said. Though you were laughing, you had tears in your eyes, and suddenly I understood that you were taking this entirely seriously. You seriously thought that something had happened. I was shocked. 'Irina,' I said. You had found a second passage, similar to the first. You were halfway through it when you threw the novel at my head. It hit me over the eye. You threw it with all your strength and it hurt. 'Why did you do that?' I shouted. 'Have you gone mad? It's just a book. It means nothing. I've helped her out. She wanted to thank me. So what? Maybe she does like me. I don't know. Morozov likes you. I don't mind. I've seen you flirting with him. It's nothing serious. If I had something to hide, why would I have left that book lying around here?' And it was true about Morozov. You did flirt with him. 'Irina,' I said. 'This is insane. She's lonely. She has no one else to turn to . . . What should I do?'

Your cigarettes were on the table. You took one and put it in your mouth. Your hands were shaking. The first match didn't work — the phosphorus smeared off like paste when you tried to strike it. When the second did the same, you threw them onto the floor. 'Stop seeing her,' you said. 'Stop seeing her.'

I picked up the matches and lit one for you. 'Okay,' I said. 'I'll stop seeing her.'

15

He is looking through the bookshelves that entirely fill one wall of the living room. When he has looked, spine by spine, through the whole expanse, he stands there with a puzzled expression on his face. Suddenly he starts to take down the volumes of the *Great Soviet Encyclopaedia*, first edition (1947). The thing he is looking for is hidden somewhere there . . . He finds it. It is a sort of exercise book, tied shut with a strip of blue satin, the meticulous letters on the front faded almost to invisibility. *Nadezhda Filippovna Podlubnaya, 1932.*

It started as a Komsomol self-improvement exercise. This is obvious from the first entry, which was written in December 1932, when she was fifteen.

Self-study
All over the Union and in countries all over the world the annual balance sheet is being drawn up. In many cities, especially in Moscow, conferences and congresses are meeting in order to review the work of the year. We too must review

what we have achieved this year, especially in our political and psychological development. We must draw up our own balance sheets.

I have had some difficult times this year but I don't regret it. The struggle has taught me a lot. It has helped me work out a new approach to life. I think this year I have arrived at a new stage of my consciousness. I have come to see my work as an integral part of my existence, as indispensable to me as the bread I need in order to live. Or even more important. It is what makes me a useful person, it is what justifies my existence. As Comrade Stalin has said, work is a matter of honour, glory, valour and heroism. I have taught myself to understand this, and now that I have understood it I will put it into practice in my life. So I am optimistic about the future.

I have to be more systematic. Sometimes I am lazy. I have to try and develop a more materialistic worldview and become more politically oriented. I get downhearted sometimes. I need to learn to have more trust in my own strength and will power. In short, I need to work on my psychology.

Positive and negative examples
A positive example is my mother. She understands the need to rework herself and learn to develop a proletarian psychology. She attends evening school and performs voluntary social work, for which she has even received awards. In the summer she went to a summer camp to cut peat. Though it was difficult, she stayed for a whole month until the victorious end. As Gorky says: 'Life is a struggle!' I admire her more than anyone else.

A negative example would be my uncle Fyodr. He is of no use to anyone and completely superfluous. He has left the old behind in many ways, but not altogether. But in the material sense definitely. Yet he hasn't been able to join the new. We have to help him with many things. We must force him to work on himself. His character is that of an old man, although he's not really very old.

Other negative examples would be the Rodins. These people who live in our flat

172

are all from a village, an extremely low milieu. For instance Vaska is only twenty and he is often dead drunk. On drunken legs he taps out a dance. He forgets that it's time to go to work and that his comrades are waiting for him, that the driver is waiting with the truck (he's a loader). He has emptied a whole bottle of vodka, he couldn't care less. But tomorrow? Tomorrow when he loses his job, and his bread? And when they won't give him work, where will he go? Perhaps he'll steal. Or he'll literally die of hunger. Without a home, he'll freeze to death. He is someone who it will be very difficult, if not impossible, to put on his feet.

Her father's name was Podlubny. He was a Ukrainian kulak, who prospered under the NEP. In 1929 the family were dekulakised, and Podlubny was sent to Arkhangelsk for a period of internal exile. Nadezhda and her mother, Yefrosinya, obtained false papers showing them to be of proletarian origin and settled in Moscow. Her mother found work as a janitor. In spite of speaking only Ukrainian and having to learn Russian as she went (when Aleksandr knew her there was no trace of this in her voice, she spoke like an educated Muscovite), she soon excelled in school. She joined the Komsomol, where she also excelled.

Living with a secret past was stressful and frightening and for the first few years her journal was full of examples of this. One summer, her Komsomol brigade organised a work trip to a *kolkhoz* near Moscow. She was one of the leaders of this initiative, and suggested that everyone get up at sunrise and work until late morning, then sleep for a few hours. Some of the others did not want to get up so early, until they understood how unpleasant it was to be in the fields in the middle of the day. Then they wondered why she was so familiar with farm life. From then on she pretended not to know what she was doing. The following winter, she and her mother met 'Vova and Itta', former neighbours from their village, on a street in Moscow. They had fled the famine in the Ukraine, and Yefrosinya helped them find shelter in the city. Nadezhda, however, shunned them, worried that they would tell people who she was.

As a teenager, she observed people intently — the secretary of the Komsomol brigade, some of her teachers and school-friends — and imitated them, trying to understand how she should look, speak, move, what opinions she should hold, and how she should express them.

I asked the leader of the political circle: what should I read first, Marx or Lenin? She said I should read both at the same time. That is very significant. She advised me to work with a pencil. In Marx, in his philosophy, he says so many obscure things, so much in it is difficult to understand, there are such depths, that you read it for the second and third time and still discover the significance of something new. You don't see everything at once. Today, in my present state of development, I understand only one part, the easiest and most obvious part. Tomorrow I will understand something new. I have also been reading novels. For instance, I've just read The Life of Klim Samgin *by Gorky.*

Over time, she started to worry less about the possibility that she might be 'unmasked' as a kulak — though she worried that if she applied for university her past would be investigated — and more about the fundamental question of her psychology. Was she psychologically healthy? In other words, did she now have a proletarian psychology? She knew that, through useful work, it was possible even for kulaks to feel their way towards this. However, she found it impossible to know for sure whether she had successfully done so. Her struggle with this was the main theme of her journal from 1934 onwards; from initial optimism — *What am I supposed to do? Well, that's obvious. I only need to perform socially useful work in a proletarian spirit* — to uncertainty — *I need to perform socially useful work in a proletarian spirit. But am I working in this spirit? How am I ever to know this?* — to fear — *So has my entire progressive development been false, superficial, no more than a mask? I lie awake at night when I think that, it sucks the blood from my stomach like the sap from a birch tree* — and despair — *It's not a question of working harder, of trying, striving. It's a question of psychology, pure and simple. I have to accept it, I have a sick psychology.*

What made her feel sure, in the summer of 1936, that she had a 'sick psychology' was an increasing sense of her own unhappiness. Psychologically healthy people are happy. That was almost a tautology. *When it is done in a proletarian spirit, work makes you happy.* One thing in

176

particular, she thought, was obstructing her path to psychological health and happiness.

To try and lead a double life, to hide my origins from people, will never succeed. It's of no use to anyone, least of all myself. The thing is, I must stop pretending to myself that this isn't the whole problem.

I have become a secretive, dishonest person, unable to speak openly. I do not have my own thoughts. I find myself parroting things that are foreign to me. Pretending to be healthy and optimistic in what I say, when I'm not.

Though she was terrified of being 'unmasked', she often fantasised about it as something that would liberate her, since she would then be able to speak 'sincerely and truthfully' to 'people who understand that my whole life is a lie'. These 'people', the people to whom she would be able to speak sincerely and truthfully, the people who would understand, were the NKVD.

Early one morning in January 1937 she and her mother were woken by a knock on the door. A police officer was there. They let him in and he searched the room. He did not say what he was looking for. Whatever it was he did not seem to find it. Then he said to Yefrosinya that she should come with him to the police station 'just for a few minutes'. She went. At nightfall there was still no sign of her.

Every morning long lines formed at the information office of the Moscow militia. Nadya stood there from four o'clock. It was snowing. Then it stopped. At eight it started to get light. When it was finally her turn at the small window, some time in the mid-afternoon, the official was unable to tell her where her mother was. In the end she managed to track her down to a Moscow prison and went to visit her there. Yefrosinya told her that she had been sentenced to eight years for using false identity papers.

She had always excelled in her school work. Now, at the Second Medical Institute, the elite university where she had won a place the previous year, her work was 'mediocre', something linked in her mind with her psychological problems. *The truth is, I am a pessimistic, negative person.* She wondered, not very seriously, whether to kill herself. Instead, in the summer of 1937, at the end of her first year at the institute, she married one of her teachers. He had been pursuing her for some time, having seen her sitting near the front in his lectures. A few men had been mentioned previously in her journal (*On the 27th I went skating with Alyosha on the skating rink of the Central House of the Red Army* . . .) but Lozovsky was the first to be written about at length. After turning down several more extravagant offers, she went to the cinema with him. *Went to the cinema with M. A film called* Modern Times. She said she had thought films were 'stupid' but that this one had been 'interesting'. Over tea in the Palace of Scientists, Lozovsky told her about Charlie Chaplin and California. Then he drove her home. Things went on like this for some time. Films, the theatre, tea. They wrote letters to each other. *You should stop hiding your feelings and emotions*, he wrote in February, in a letter which she transcribed to her journal. *You are lonely, and that is because you want very much, but are not willing to give anything in return.*

In the late thirties, Lozovsky had a moustache. Aleksandr knows this from the photographs that were found in the house at Metelyev Log. In those photographs it was possible to see the extent to which her life must have been transformed when she married him. (The very existence of so many photographs, of course, was evidence of this.) Lozovsky's flat was quiet, light, with parquet floors and space for an imported piano. He was one of the intellectual luminaries of the Soviet Union — a sort of prodigy, not yet forty and the head of the Second Medical Institute, winner of a Stalin Prize and 50,000 roubles in the year of his wedding. (Nadya's mother had earned 2,400 roubles a year as a janitor.) He was handsome, athletic — there were photos of him in tennis whites, and showing off on skates — and he lived a life of extreme privilege. Foreign tailoring, perfumed soap, special food packages. Weekends at the house in Uspenskoye, skiing and skating in the winter. Visits to the Barvikha sanatorium. Summer holidays in the Crimea, where the Academy of Sciences maintained the Gaspra estate for its most eminent members.

She still studied at the institute, took the tram there, had lunch in the student dining hall. In 1940 she qualified as a doctor — with high marks, she exaggerated when she said her work was 'mediocre' — and started to practise. In 1941, they moved to Sverdlovsk. Her journal entries of those years, far fewer than previously, are no more than short notes of events — *Suvorovs to dinner, Sent parcel to Mama* — and even these end in 1944, when they moved to Metelyev Log. There is one more entry, written in pencil on the final page of the journal and undated.

I am by nature a pessimistic person. I do not have a naturally progressive or optimistic — 'proletarian' — spirit. Of course, I know I should be working, should be trying to be of use to people. I just don't seem to have the strength. The strength of spirit more than the physical strength. Life often seems meaningless to me. Isn't that a terrible thing to say? Here it's easier to ignore that. You can lose sight of it when you spend so much time alone, when you spend so much time in nature. Maybe that's why I like it here. It's only because I've failed so totally elsewhere that I like it here. It's a matter of weakness, of withdrawal, surrender, failure. I know that. For weeks at a time, I am able to ignore this. Then I wake up in the middle of the night, and I know that's what it is. At those moments I wonder whether I should kill myself straight away, without hesitation, without letting myself think my way out of it. My whole life seems such a sad and stupid waste.

It frightens me to think how much time has passed. When I think of the past, I think, 'If I'd known then I'd end up like this . . . ' There's something so sad about that thought.

I must stop this now. I can't stand the sound of this stupid voice prattling in my head. All it shows is what a mess I've made of my life.

When he read this for the first time in 1948, lying on the chaise longue in his office, he felt that it was addressed to him personally, that it was a plea for his help, and he hoped that he would be able to help her, psychologically and politically as well as practically. That, he now understands, was naïve.

And what would it mean in practice anyway?

A lot of talk. He did not tell her that he had read her journal. Instead he used his own life as an example. He told her that his father had been a kulak. (Very few people knew this — only those who had known him since his school-days.) Psychology was not necessarily hereditary. He told her a story he had told no one else. In 1920 — or was it 1921? — one afternoon in September, he and his father had dug a pit in a spinney a few versts from the village. A pit for a hiding place. It was narrow at the top and wider further down, like a jug, and they dried the earth with smoke from smouldering straw. To dig the pit and dry it took two whole days. Then they lowered sacks of grain and potatoes in, laid more straw on top and plugged the entrance with wet, sticky soil. Though he did not understand exactly why they were doing this — he was only eight years old — he felt very proud of his father. It was obvious from his satisfied smile that he — *they!* — had outsmarted someone. Even Ivan did not know about that. At the time, he told her, he had thought that his life would be more or less identical to his father's. Everyone had it in them to escape the past. He himself was proof of it. And since it was possible, it was also necessary. Not that it was easy.

He told her the story of Zinaida Denisevskaya. She was one of the teachers at the school in Basmanovo where he went until he left for Sverdlovsk in 1924. Later, she also moved to Sverdlovsk, and worked first in the city library, and then as a scientist at an experimental poultry farm in the suburbs. She was, he said, a typical product of the pre-Revolutionary provincial intelligentsia. Unlike the other teacher at the Basmanovo school, Evdokimov, she was not a Communist. At first she sympathised with the Revolution as a liberal, but soon she found that the Bolshevik state offended her petit bourgeois sensibilities — her father had been the headmaster of a private girls' school. The pupils sensed the tension between herself and Evdokimov on

183

this point. She was physically frail but she had a strong will and she did not want him to teach them to be little Bolsheviks. She wanted to make them in her own image — that is, the image of the bourgeois liberal, something out of Chekhov, the worried doctor, the conscience-stricken schoolteacher. To Aleksandr, she always seemed sad — a small woman in a straw hat, with a sharp face, and a sharp tongue. Then, in the summer of 1924, she got ill. He was not sure what it was — perhaps yellow fever. She stopped teaching. They were told that she was dying, and when he left for Sverdlovsk in September, he thought that she was dead.

He was therefore surprised to see her name on a list in the city morgue years later, in 1937. He found out when the funeral was, and went. It was her. She had survived yellow fever in 1924, and died of leukaemia in 1937. There were only two of them at the funeral, himself and a young female teacher from the Urals Agricultural Institute, where Denisevskaya had been working when she died. He wanted to know what had happened to her since Basmanovo so he went to the institute to look at her possessions. There, he found her diaries, thousands of pages of them.

In 1925, when she moved to Sverdlovsk

and found work at the city library, she was very lonely. *The main thing I lack is love*, she wrote. *That is why I have nothing to write about.* Eventually, in the late twenties, she moved to the experimental poultry farm, where she lived and worked for most of the rest of her life. Initially she hated it there. She described it as a 'swamp', the only 'island of civilisation' the home of the director and his wife, the Ferdinandovs, where she had her small room. When these people were transferred to a veterinary institute in Sverdlovsk she wrote that she was losing her only friends, and with them her only pleasures in life, their piano playing and educated talk. However, in time she started to value her younger fellow workers more. She noted their strength of mind, practical orientation and unshakeable optimism. Of her new assistant, Antonina, she said, *She is a new type, intensely living, some sort of new woman.* And a few months later: *She is the true heir to what I valued and loved about the Russian intelligentsia.* When she visited the Ferdinandovs in Sverdlovsk, she found that the old warmth was no longer there. *I am amazed by their narrow personal outlook on life. If there is no white bread or no white cloth it means life is terrible. The fact that other people's lives have improved is not* taken into account. *They sneer at everything, speak ironically about everything. It's tiresome, this endless hostility towards everything.*

She was then in the midst of a love affair, possibly the first and only one of her life. Her lover, Alyosha, was twenty years younger than she was. When it started, in the autumn of 1929, she was forty and he was twenty. In December, he left to study in Moscow, and they wrote letters to each other. Alyosha wrote that he still loved her and that she meant everything to him. To prove it, he said that he was unable to stop masturbating when he thought of her. She found his earthiness off-putting. Her letters to him were patronising. She lectured him on the infinite distance that separated his 'physiological urges' from 'spiritual love'. In these letters, Aleksandr heard the voice of the Denisevskaya he had known himself, the village schoolteacher. This, for instance: *For once in your life please write me a sensible, detailed, sincere letter. Only this will decide what form our relations assume in the future. Don't rush, it would be better to write the letter over several days.* In writing to each other, Alyosha used the formal pronoun, she the informal.

When he visited her the next summer, she wrote in her diary that she found him

186

tedious, with nothing interesting to say about Moscow. When he left she wrote, *I miss him extremely*. She did not see him for more than a year. Then, one day in the summer of 1931, he proposed to her. She turned him down. *The way he nods when he says goodbye, his maladroitness, his way of speaking — it makes me want to weep for him, and for me.* That was in her diary. To him she wrote, *It is very painful to say this but, although you are sincere and pure, you are not as I would like you to be.*

In October, he proposed again. They were married. He was by then a party official and often away. She wrote him long letters. *I am older than you and therefore more demanding in love than you are. I want more sincere feelings, more profound joys, more mutual nurturing than the two of us are experiencing* ... He wrote her short notes and postcards. *He doesn't know how to love,* she said. She ended the marriage in 1933. Later, thinking about it, she said that Alyosha was a *man of the modern style*, and what she wanted from him was therefore *historically impossible*. From this historical perspective, she saw that she had misunderstood him, that his idiom, which she had thought an obstacle to personal expression and intimacy, was in fact his natural language, the sober and factual language of modern times. She started to see herself, too, in this historical perspective — *I have found a new world for me in Marxism* — positioned between the obsolete old world and the emerging new one, part of neither. This, she said, explained her lifelong loneliness:

In the last years of her life, she was a fervent supporter of the *kolkhoz* system. Of one such farm she said, *I was there for only five days but it seemed that I saw a new world. I know that in different places different things are happening — including some terrible things — but it makes me so happy to know that mankind has set out on the right path. We will have a new life, and new people.* Even then she wrestled with the legacy of her education, and she still felt *unable to march with the new generation.* This was not just a metaphor. She longed to take part in the marches and parades that she saw — or, isolated on the farm as she was, more often heard on the radio. On May Day 1936, she wrote, *Yesterday I was sad that I knew no one I could visit for the holiday, but today I was among my own family* — on Red *Square in Moscow, at the People's Palace in Voronezh, in Baku, Kiev and other places. For the whole day I have been in touch with the holiday through the radio. For the whole* day *I have not felt alone.*

In February 1937, she was transferred from the farm to the Urals Agricultural Institute in Sverdlovsk, where she lectured on subjects such as 'the dialectics of the poultry egg'. Her workload was heavy, and her health was poor. Then on May Day she celebrated with students and teachers from all over the city, and for the first time in her life she marched in the parade.

Yesterday — an evening meeting in the barracks. Today — the parade. Exhaustion hampers my feelings of joy. But more important is the sense of merging with everybody who celebrated this day. All of us, our institute, all the other institutes, the workers' faculties and schools, all the workers, all the Red Army soldiers, all of us — were one. We all marched together — with the same songs and thoughts. This time I did not see the 'face of the people', because I myself was part of it, I was a drop in the sea, I was forming the '1st of May', and wasn't just an onlooker. I'm extremely tired. First we waited for three hours, then we marched quickly. I almost got sick. I hardly managed to get home but I am happy to have done this. Perhaps this was the first and last time I will participate in a parade.

When she took part in this parade Denisevskaya was dying. She died only a few months later, and this is one of the final entries in her diary. Aleksandr sent it to the Sverdlovsk Library, with this note: *Please find enclosed the diary of Zinaida Denisevskaya, who once worked at your library. I think it is worth preserving for posterity. It is the story of a lifelong struggle, with loneliness, with social isolation, with political error. However, when you read the final entries your heart overflows with joy. You see how the face of this person lights up, the face of a Soviet person, who was deeply passionate about educating the liberated people, the makers of a new life — and finally, in the supreme moment of her own existence, on May Day 1937, she herself was one of them, and she made a new life.*

When he went to see her in the flat on Karl Libknekht Street, the talk often moved to politics, history, philosophy. Sometimes it was very earnest. Sometimes it had the quality of intellectual play — like her husband, she enjoyed this, and took the sparring seriously. Usually she made tea. They sat at Shtern's

190

table, sipping this tea and trying to find the tone — easy, flowing, languorous, with no particular purpose, full of silences — that had made the endless wet afternoons at Metelyev Log what they were. When he thought of those afternoons, he thought of her leaning on the pine dresser, smoking, her face turned to the windows, and the smoke from her papirosa swimming listlessly towards them. The rain falling steadily. Time was so extended, so open-ended. There seemed to be no sort of external pressure at all.

In Sverdlovsk, when he went to see her, it was not like that. Not that it was tense or stilted. It was not. It simply lacked the sense of taking place in an isolated oxbow of time. No-particular-purpose did not seem as permissible as it had in the oxbow. Silences seemed to be minor problems when someone would eventually leave, when time was limited, when they were together not simply because that was how things inescapably were, but with a specific intention — though sometimes, sitting there, it was not obvious to him what that intention was. Sometimes, when the silence settled, even for only a few seconds, while she sat opposite him, smoke wreathing her tired face, he would think, *What am I doing here? I'll leave when I've finished this tea.* And even look forward to

191

leaving. Then the silence would pass — some-one would say something — and two hours later he would still be there.

Once or twice a week he took her to the baths, signing her in to the First Department, and waiting for her in the foyer afterwards, his skin still tingling from the *banya*. Waiting there, he was always nervous — as he was wherever he went with her — that someone he knew would see him, so he waited to the side, near one of the pillars, shielding his face with a newspaper. Not that he had anything to hide. It was then that they usually went to the Ural for lunch. There too he worried that they would be seen. He always asked for the same table, near the kitchen, and sat with his back to the room, not suspecting that the waitress serving them their soup and *kotleta* was more of a threat to his secret — though what in fact was secret? — than the procuracy official he vaguely knew who was lunching with a judge at the window table.

He walked her to Karl Libknekht Street after lunch. It took ten minutes. Those walks, in the pale autumn light, were melancholy. The afternoons were noticeably shortening. The sunlight shone through thinning trees. He left her at the door of the house, and went on to the MGB offices on his own.

16

You know what happens now. The note from Nikita Stepanovich. He said he wanted to see me about something important, and knocked on the door in the early evening, just when I was starting to wonder where you were. 'Nikita!' I said. I had not seen him for over a year, not since Epshteyn's funeral. I was surprised how much weight he had put on, even since then, though of course he was very stocky and muscular in his youth, and men like that often turn obese later.

Still wheezing from the stairs, he took off his hat — there wasn't much hair left underneath it — and I helped him out of his wet raincoat. He loosened the collar of his white shirt. His manner was very serious and unsmiling.

'How are you?' I said.

'I'm okay.'

He did not seem to want to spend time on pleasantries, so I said, 'What is it? What can I do for you?'

'Irishka's left,' he said.

'What?'

He sighed. 'She's left.'

'What are you talking about?'

'She's moved in with us.' Sweating nervously, he wiped his face with a handkerchief. 'I know it's not a nice thing to have to tell you — '

'What are you talking about? What's going on?'

'I think you know what.'

'No, I don't.'

'You've been seeing someone else.'

'What?'

'You heard me.'

'What are you talking about?' I shouted. 'Where's Irina?'

'Oh stop it. There's no point.'

'Where is she?'

'She's at my house,' he snapped. 'And I might be angry too, Sasha. She is my sister . . . '

'What has she told you?'

'It's not what she's told me. I've seen it with my own eyes.'

'What?'

'I've seen it with my own eyes.'

'Seen what? What have you seen?'

'I've seen you with her. With Lozovskaya.' He thought he had me. I must have looked shocked. I was shocked — I was shocked that he knew the name. I had not told you the name. 'What do you mean?' I said.

'I've been watching you. Irishka said she

suspected something. She asked me to look into it.'

'Look into what?'

'Your involvement with Lozovskaya. Why deny it? It just makes you look silly.'

'Deny what?'

'A few days ago,' he said, slightly shame-faced, 'I followed you when you left work . . . '

'You followed me?'

'I followed you. Yes. I followed you. I'm sorry. Irishka said she suspected something. So I followed you. You went to a flat on Karl Libknekht Street. You were there for an hour or two. I waited outside. When you left, I went in and spoke to some of the neighbours. They said you were there virtually every day . . . '

'That isn't true.'

'That you were sometimes there in the evenings. That you sometimes went out with her. I had a photo of you — they identified you.'

'This is a joke . . . '

'Is it? They said the room she lives in was formerly occupied by a man called Shtern, who was arrested last month. They said you moved her in soon after. I didn't think you did things like that, Sasha.'

'Like what?'

'You know what I mean. They say you take

her presents. Scent. Underwear. Shoes. They say you're her lover. They're sure of it.' He shrugged. 'It's obvious. Why deny it?'

'It's not true!'

'I've seen it with my own eyes.'

'Seen WHAT?'

'That you practically live there!'

'You've seen nothing!'

'Several times I've seen you spend hours in there.'

'There's nothing to see!'

'Do you think I'm an idiot?' he shouted. 'Do you think I'm a total idiot?'

'I want you to leave! Leave!'

We stared at each other. Then, slowly, he stood up and took his things. He sighed sadly. 'Will you come and speak to her?' he said. 'Maybe if you say you're sorry . . . '

'No! I'm not sorry. I've done nothing. She should be sorry, for spying on me! And you should be sorry!' I was shouting, following him out into the hall. Zalesky and his family were sitting down to supper in the kitchen. They pretended not to notice us. Nikita was obviously embarrassed to be part of this scene. He edged his way out, holding his hat.

He was there again a few days later. You know that — you sent him. 'We were expecting you,' he said.

'Why?' I said. 'I told you. I've done nothing.'

He nodded, putting some of your underwear into a holdall. 'Still, we were expecting you . . . '

'YOU were?'

'Irishka was . . . '

That's what he said. You were expecting me! What for? You were the one who had walked out! You walked out on me without saying a word. What were you expecting me for?

I said to Nikita, 'How long is she planning to stay with you?'

He shut the holdall and shrugged. 'I don't know. She can stay for as long as she likes.'

'Why is she staying with you?' I said. 'I don't understand.'

'We're waiting for you,' he said.

A week later he was there again. 'Listen,' he said. 'Just say you're sorry. Is that too much to ask?'

'Sorry for what?'

He shut his eyes sanctimoniously. 'Just say you're sorry . . . '

'I've done nothing to be sorry for!'

'If you say you're sorry — and obviously stop seeing this woman — things might be okay.'

'Might they?'

'You look terrible, Sasha,' he said. 'I want to help you patch things up. That's why I'm here.'

'If you want to help patch things up, tell

197

your stupid sister to stop being so stupid.'
'Don't talk about Irishka like that,' he said.
And I said, 'Fuck you.'
When he had left I started to drink.

17

He has hugely overslept. It is nearly eight. The electric light is still on in the kitchen, and the bottle of Ararat Armenian *konyak* still on the table. He is surprised how little of it there is left. He was sure there was more than a few meagre millimetres of the stuff when he went to sleep — something of which he has no memory. For a minute, not used to the pain, he tries to pretend that it is a normal morning. He lights the stove, the hissing blue teeth, sets the pan over it to make his tea . . . No. No, it is not working. The hangover is like an intimation of mortality. It is like a foretaste of the pain of the last illness, when — in the fire of whatever it is that is killing him — he will find death preferable to persisting in this world, though it is surely the only world there is. He extinguishes the stove — silences its tiny hiss, which was hurting his head — and shuffles into the still shrouded bedroom. Lying there in a tight foetal position, in time the pain dies down to a quiet flame, only licking his outline. If he stays totally still for long enough it will slowly sink to a mere ember. There is a profound vacancy in his head. No thoughts, no memories. Perhaps this is the oblivion the *konyak* promised, the only sound the tired jostle of his own heart.

He sleeps until the early afternoon. Then — feeling spectral, weightless — he wanders into the living room. Steady rain is blackening the stout boughs of the cherry tree, the leaves of which are starting to fade and fall. He switches on the radio. The news. Kissinger is in Moscow — his wailing motorcade is just leaving the airport. The news-reader says he is there to talk about nuclear disarmament and Vietnam — Le Duc Tho is also in town — and trade. *Trade. In other words, the integration of the USSR into the international financial system, as a prelude to the reintroduction of free market principles to the Soviet economy* . . . Still very hungover, he does not feel strong enough to face this sort of thing, and switches off the radio, interrupting the next news item — '*For a second day, Israeli aircraft have attacked targets in Syria and* — '

In the near-silence — there is only the quiet sound of the rain — he pulls the page from the typewriter. The last words he typed were *When he had left I started to drink.* That was what had inspired him to take the *konyak* from the top shelf, where it had stood for so many years. He pours what is left of it down the sink. *When he had left* . . . Nikita Stepanovich. Dead. Heart attack. 1965. Once, in their early teens, they were inseparable friends. Nikita was one of the other 'Epshteynites'. Aleksandr has no memory of their first meeting — it would have happened in September 1924. Even the idea of 'their first meeting' seems strange to him. It is more or less impossible, now, for him to imagine himself in his former state of not-knowing-Nikita. His former state. He saw Sverdlovsk for the first time on an autumn afternoon of perpetual twilight. He had never seen so many people and horses. He had never seen electric light. Most of the pupils were the sons of industrial workers, and they seemed like hostile foreigners to him. When he thought of the house in the village, of the earthen floor where he slept with Ivan, on a straw-filled mattress in summer and sheepskins in winter, he had to hide his tears. The school was warm and there was always enough to eat. The teachers were mostly tough men — some of them, like Epshteyn, veterans of the Civil War, though mostly without Epshteyn's intellect. The emphasis was not so much on intellectual excellence as the inculcation of an ethos, and in this environment differences were quickly effaced as the shared experience of the school shaped all the pupils in the same way. The way they spoke, for instance. Surprisingly quickly, the peasants' sons lost their old ways of speaking. They spoke like their urban peers, and used their slang. Within a few months it was impossible to tell them apart, and Aleksandr felt more at home with Nikita Stepanovich's family, with whom he spent the holidays, than with his own.

There were four sisters, and it was one of the others — he sometimes forgets this — with whom he was infatuated for several years in his teens. She was older than him, and when he heard of her engagement to an engine driver he thought his life was over. She went to live in Novosibirsk and he soon forgot her.

His first specific memory of Irina. She is wearing a white shift, like a nightdress. Her father was a shock-worker, and the family had their own flat in a new development near the machine factory, Uralmash. The development was designed by a famous German architect who inspected it one day, passing along the plain corridors in his Homburg, surrounded by officials. He stood in the living room of the flat, putting questions to Irina's father through an interpreter. Irina was there, ignoring Aleksandr, who was ignoring her. What they did together was still a secret from her family. She had instigated it, one afternoon when they were alone in the flat. Unlike him, she was not a virgin.

In October he went to Moscow to study law at the OGPU Higher School. Everyone was impressed that he had won a place there. There was a party the night before he left, and in the morning she went with him to the station. No one had seen him off from a station since his mother, from the tiny wind-tousled platform at Basmanovo in 1924. Wet snow was falling, melting on the tall black locomotive. Wet feet left prints in the pale slush. He told her not to wait. She was wet and shivering. He kissed her the way he had seen people kissing in films — her face was numb — and settled himself in the train. Then, when it started to move, he heard her voice shouting 'Sasha!' and shoved down the window.

Sasha!
Sasha!
She was there, on the platform, trying to keep pace with the train. She had waited, and more than forty years later the sound of her voice is present to his mind with such untarnished precision that it seems it has only just stopped.

Sasha!
He stayed at the open window, with his

203

face in the wind, until one of the other passengers — he had forgotten about them — told him to shut it. Which he did, and sat down wiping his eyes on his sleeve.

There was then, in 1930, a sense of excitement about everything. Following the slow, tactical twenties it seemed that the Revolution was finally under way, with the end of private manufacturing and trade, the industrialisation of the first Five Year Plan, the establishment of the *kolkhoz* system, and the formation of a new Soviet working-class intelligentsia, of which he was so proud to be a member. All these things seemed to be happening with a sudden unstoppable momentum, while the imperialist world staggered through the slump that would destroy its unjust economic structure.

Sinyavsky, the head of the OGPU Higher School, was addressing the students in the summer of 1932. It was the end of the university year, a hot June day. The sunny gymnasium was full of students in their white cadets' uniforms. Sinyavsky, also in uniform, was unusually solemn. 'The Civil War,' he said, 'did not end in 1921 — it did not end at all. It is well known that after their defeat many Whites, those who could not escape abroad, pretended to be Communists, and entered the state, party, and security services, especially in places far from Moscow. They never truly accepted their defeat, and they never lost their old loyalties. So among the millions of people who participated in the victorious struggle to overthrow the tsar, and who joined the Communist Party, there were, unfortunately, some who did so for reasons other than fighting for the proletariat and for Communism, and in time a number of these people found themselves in important positions in the party, the state and the armed forces.' Sinyavsky paused, and surveyed the several hundred young, serious faces in front of him, among them Aleksandr's, near the front, the wool of his uniform prickling his neck in the heat. 'In the twenties,' Sinyavsky went on, 'they tried to achieve their ends through politics, these people, the Rightists. They even tried to take control of the party and its policies. They failed in this. Now they have turned to more desperate methods — to wrecking, violence, murder, terrorism. What they tried to achieve through politics in the past, they now try to achieve through violence. This is the new situation.' They listened in sober silence while he listed the plots that had been foiled that year, all of them involving party members, some even members of the

Central Committee. The Riutin conspiracy, the Eismont-Tolmachev-Smirnov conspiracy, Trotsky's conspiracies with his supporters still in the USSR — such as Radek, Smilga and Preobrazhensky — and his letter to the Central Committee, written from his hiding place in Mexico, in which he explicitly threatened the Soviet state with terrorist violence.

★ ★ ★

He was always surprised, when he saw her for the first time from the still-just-moving train, waiting for him in the humid June air or the fog of December, how pretty she was. Her smile. Her slightly Asiatic eyes. Asiatic in shape — they were blue. It was somehow strange to see her there. The first time, he did not know what to expect. There was a sort of trepidation. They eyed each other like strangers on the icy platform. Kissed on the mouth with a sort of formality. They had written to each other — passionate, unwary letters — which only made it stranger to be warily face to face, pink-nosed, and not quite as they were in their memories of each other. Her eyes were watering in the frozen air. She laughed. 'What?' he said. It was mid-afternoon. She had left work early. The flat was empty and as soon as the door was shut they tumbled fumbling onto the floor. With her skirt around her waist she was still wearing her winter coat and scarf, though her hat had fallen off. They were lucky that the flat was empty — it was the school holidays and her grandmother had taken the younger siblings skating. There was a scarcity of solitude.

In summer, of course, there was outdoors. There was the path, usually unnoticed, to the side of the Uspenskaya Church, shrunk to little more than a parting in the vegetation, variegated with warm white blotches of sunlight. It led to a stream, which in turn flowed under foliage into the Iset a few kilometres south of the town, where, though wide, it slid in whispering shallows over stones.

In winter it was less easy to find places. Once they used the nightwatchman's hut of a warehouse which was shut for the New Year holiday. The nightwatchman was her uncle, and was away for a few days. The weather was mild, unsettled, overcast. A midwinter thaw. Inside, the hut was filthy and extremely damp, infested with woodlice and spiders. In the night the sleet drummed on the old newspaper over the window. In the morning there were human voices in the street outside.

They slept pressed together in the valley of the mattress.

★ ★ ★

He finds the photograph of her which he took to Moscow — a smiling studio shot — in an old envelope. (On the envelope is written, in her handwriting, his name and the words, *Feliks Dzerzhinsky Higher School, 48 Pelshe Street, Moscow.* For a few moments he stares at those words. They are extraordinarily evocative, more so even than the photograph itself. They make him sigh tearfully. She had the elegant handwriting of the semi-educated. Her father, though a Communist, had old-fashioned ideas on subjects such as the education of women, and she left school at eleven. Her mother was illiterate.) There are other photographs in the envelope. The wedding photo from 1934, unframed, and stored as mere memorabilia — he in his new NKVD lieutenant's uniform, twenty-two years old, black-haired, staring into the camera with an intently serious expression. And Irina, smiling, holding her lilies. The photographer was striving for the tone of the silver screen, fussing with props and silk flowers. (Irina's lilies were made of silk.) Aleksandr was impatient with him. The photographer understood what he was making though — understood that a wedding photo is not so much a memory as an idea. That it must transcend the sharp toxic smells of the studio, the oppressive summer heat, the struggle of the fly on the skylight. That it is in fact a symbol of such transcendence, no less an instrument of faith than the sooty ikons of Aleksandr's faint memories of his parents' house, or the portraits of Lenin in every public place.

The wedding party was held in the officers' mess of the NKVD headquarters. General Reshetov sent flowers. Of Aleksandr's family, only Ivan was there — a high-spirited seventeen-year-old wearing a suit for the first time. He and Nikita Stepanovich, who had just qualified as an engineer from the Urals State Technical University, were his witnesses.

They lived first with Irina's parents. A fractious period, but one which time has endowed with a sort of purity, a prelapsarian shine. It was not until two years later that they moved into the flat on Malyshev Street — he is looking at a photo of Irina standing outside it, some time in the late thirties, shielding her eyes with her hand. Their room had a marble fireplace, the flue stuffed with old newspaper, and a long squat radiator under the window, which in winter emitted sullen heat and the smell of scorched paint. He sees them on their first night there, half-undressed in the laughable luxury of their own space; he is teaching her how to play chess — how to set out the pieces, how each piece moves, the significance of the king.

18

It was — what? A week, ten days, since you had left. It seemed like much longer. I lived through that terrible week moment by moment, and only as I drove out to the smoggy suburb did I understand what a torment it had been. A state of permanent enervation. There was no variation in it, only the same few thoughts and feelings, turning like a sluggish whirlpool. Eventually, there was nothing I would not do to escape it. Sleepless, undernourished, nearly losing my mind, I pushed the service Pobeda through the quagmire of autumn.

Nikita's house was an odd thing, wasn't it. A little low house surrounded, first, by a picket fence — within which there was that sad, sooty garden — and then by the huge structures of the steelworks. Towering smoke-stacks. Pipelines. Furnaces. Slagheaps. Maybe it wasn't quite like that. That's how it is in my memory though.

Fine rain was falling that morning. The house was streaked with wet soot, and its windows were veiled with the stuff so that the light inside was dim and dirty. We stood in the parlour, in that light. There was no one else there. The family were all at work or school. I told you, for the umpteenth time, that nothing had happened, whatever Nikita might say. It was true that I still sometimes went to see her. She had written to me. She was lonely. I felt sorry for her. I went to see her. That was true . . . It was all very familiar.

And then I said something else. Something I had not envisaged saying. Not for a second. I said, 'I think I might be in love with her.'

Silence.

Quiet pattering on smutty windowpanes.

It was a moment that would have been unimaginable only a few months earlier, perhaps only a few weeks earlier. I think you were shocked. Though you had never accepted my protestations of innocence, I suppose you had hoped they were true. And they were. That was the point.

You sighed — a spontaneous open-mouthed sigh, almost a sob — and there was another of those long silences, in the middle of which the lifeless objects of the parlour — the maid's mattress, the table, the black iron taps — seemed to take on a more intense existence. There were moments when I was intensely aware of them, and moments when I was not aware of them at all, as if we were standing in a pale void. 'I'm sorry,' I said.

Suddenly you shouted, 'Why do you think you can come here and talk to me like this?'

I shook my head. 'I don't know,' I said. 'I'm sorry . . . '

'Stop saying that!' You were in tears now, shouting at me. I've forgotten what you said. I was in shock too, wondering what I had done. Words are deeds. And then you were wiping your eyes and saying, 'I think you should leave now.'

'Irina . . . '

'Please, leave.'

With trembling hands I started the Pobeda, and spent the next hour taking wrong turnings, not knowing where I was, more and more lost in that smoking volcanic landscape. I don't know how I spent the next ten hours. I met Zalesky on the stairs in the twilight. He was on his way out. 'You alright?' he said, looking worriedly into my tear-stained eyes, which he would not have been able to see very well in the murky light.

I tried to smile. 'Yes. Fine. You?' He was in uniform. 'Working nights?'

'The whole week,' he said. 'It's messing me up.'

'Well . . . ' I did not know what to say. I felt no sympathy for him. 'You'll get a few days off at the end of it.'

'Yeah, just when I've got used to it.'

I went upstairs and lay on the divan for a while.

Then I went out again.

Irishka, I want to tell you something now. Something that has weighed on my mind all these years. It's important that I tell you. That evening I went to see her. It was as if a sort of darkness had opened in front of me. I don't know how else to put it.

I went to see her. 'Oh, it's you,' she said, when she opened the door. Her face was swollen. She had been asleep. She was not expecting me. I slumped down on the sofa, still in my wet coat.

'You look upset,' she said.

'I am.'

'Why?'

I did not tell her about our meeting. I never told her much about us.

She went to the kitchen. While she was away I listened to the rain on the window, or something like that. The food was from the ministry store. I said I didn't want any. Instead, I quoted Hamlet, the original bourgeois nihilist! I said, 'How weary, stale, flat, and unprofitable seem to me all the uses of this world!' She knew the lines — knew them so well in fact that she joined in from 'seem to me all the uses of this world!' You would have laughed at us, Irishka. 'I don't know what's wrong with me,' I said, laughing. 'That I feel like Hamlet. It's shameful.'

It was late. The electric light sank to an orange glow and then went out. I was still there, on the sofa, and the rain was still spilling down in the street, so she said, 'Do you want to stay the night?' I had never stayed the night until then. No, I had not. Every night since you went to Nikita's, I had slept, or not slept, alone on our divan.

'Well . . . ' I said.

'You can sleep on the sofa,' said her voice in the dark.

'Are you sure?'

'Of course.'

'Well . . . ' I sounded doubtful.

'You'll get soaked.'

'Yes. Okay. Thank you.'

I was slowly unlacing my shoes, when she said, 'Did you look at my journal?'

'No.'

'None of it?'

'No.'

I took off my shoes.

'I wrote some terrible things in it,' she said.

'Did you?'

'Yes.'

I did not know what to say. Finally I just said, 'night,' and lay down on the sofa with my overcoat on top of me.

It was totally dark. For a few minutes I heard her moving around, undressing, then the soft squeak of the bedsprings, then only the sounds of the rain. It seemed that nothing would happen that night — and if nothing happened that night, it seemed unlikely that it ever would. I was pleased. Truly. All the stress of the previous few hours — of the previous few weeks — immediately sank away, like water out of a sink. I was exhausted. I just wanted to sleep. And I did sleep, though the sofa was lumpy.

Irishka, I woke to find her sitting there with her hip pressing against my leg. She seemed to be sitting sideways, looking down at me. The rain had stopped. The silence was intense. For a few moments I did not know where I was. I had been dreaming something, and seemed suddenly to have woken. I don't know how long she had been sitting there, or how long I had been asleep.

'I know you looked at it,' she whispered.

Somehow, in the otherwise total disorientation of waking, I immediately knew what she was talking about. 'Yes, I did,' I said.

'I know. And you don't hate me for it?'

It took me a moment to understand that this was a question. 'No.'

For what seemed like a long time she sat there in silence. It was too dark for me to see her face. Then she leaned towards me and kissed me on the forehead. As soon as she had done this, she stood up and a second later I heard the squeak of the bedsprings.

Only then did it occur to me that she might have expected a warmer welcome, perched on the sofa in the middle of the night, with her hip or thigh pressing against my leg. She had sat there, it now struck me, for several minutes, as if waiting for something, and I had not moved. Maybe you will smile at this, Irishka. Please smile at it! Even when she leaned down and kissed my forehead, and her falling hair tickled my face, I had not so much as moved.

Making no effort to be quiet — quite the opposite — I pulled myself into a sitting position, and for a minute or two I sat there, as she had, on the edge of the sofa. Then, stepping slowly through the darkness, I went and stood over her. I stood there for a long time, listening to the silence, which seemed to paralyse me. It was as if I might have stood there forever. 'Are you asleep?' I said finally. She said nothing, and did not move. 'Nadya?' When she still said nothing, still did not move, I put out my hand. I was further from the bed than I had thought.

I want to tell you everything, and I will. As soon as I touched her, on the shoulder I think, she sat up violently. I thought she was going to hit me, until the unexpected presence of her tongue in my mouth made me think otherwise. I toppled over and lay on the floor underneath her. That went on for a few minutes. Then quite suddenly, it stopped. She stood up and pulled her nightdress over her head. Then, while she waited, I undressed — there was some precarious hopping as I took my trousers off, some fiddling with stubborn shirt buttons. I'm sorry to say I did not take off my socks — I thought I had kept her waiting long enough — and wearing only those not very fresh socks, with my hands I found her in the dark. And there was a surprising lot of her to find. She was a tall woman, and I was used to your small limbs.

You should laugh at what follows, Irishka. The slightest movement on that mattress produced a loud squeaking of the springs, and the walls were thin. We struggled to stay quiet. It wasn't possible of course. We even fell off the bed and landed on the floor with a thud that must have woken the whole flat. For a while, we tried to press on as though nothing had happened, until eventually she whispered, 'Wait!' and we stopped, and stood up, and felt our way wearily back onto the mattress, which sagged like a hammock. When the squeaking eventually stopped, I fell into a sweaty sleep.

In the morning it was snowing. The first snow of autumn. Huge flakes like white hens' feathers silently filling the windless air. The snow increased the strangeness of the situation, the strangeness of the warmth of another woman. Until then I had known only you. Watching it fall, I thought of you — thought of the same snow falling where you were — of you watching it fall. I did not understand what had happened. I turned from the window and saw that she had woken up. Lying on the bed under a single sheet, she was watching me. The snowlight made soft pale shadows. With a strange sort of shyness, she wrapped herself in the sheet and took the few steps to the table for her cigarettes. Later I dressed while she made tea. We sat in silence, drinking it. Outside the falling snowflakes were smaller and flurrying. When the tea was finished, I left.

★ ★ ★

I did not see you that day, as I had said I would. For a week I was not able to face you. That was when the final estrangement took place. Then there was only logistics. The work of taking things apart. A week or two later, you and Nikita turned up one morning in a truck, splashing through the flooded potholes of Malyshev Street. I suspect it was Nikita who insisted that you take everything. When it was finished, he left, wiping his hands, sweating in his shirt. You were still taking a last look, making sure nothing had been forgotten, or perhaps just lingering in the room where you had lived for so many years. Places like that are transfigured when you know you are leaving them for the last time. For a moment, they seem new again.

We went down the stairs in silence. On the landing you stopped. 'Irina . . . ' I said. I see your face now, my love — one side of it in shadow, the other in the light from the window, lined with tears. They weren't for me. I know what they were for. They were for the memory of a dead idea. We had lost faith in the idea of our life together. Unfortunately, Irishka, the process of losing faith in something, once it has started, is not easy to stop. Perhaps only a major sacrifice will do it. A sacrifice is always a sort of assertion. It's obvious what I would have to have sacrificed. What you would have had to sacrifice I don't know. You wiped the tears impatiently from your face. It was the last time we were alone together, on the landing, in the wet-plaster smell of the stairwell, next to the huge window which overlooked the yard. 'It's okay,' you said, and we went down the last flight of stairs and out into the street.

When I went up on my own — my legs were trembling — it seemed strange that only a few minutes earlier you had been standing there, on the landing, wiping your eyes. And now this was over.

19

For the next two weeks, when he finished work, he walked to Karl Libknekht Street through the shortening twilight and looked up at the light in the second-floor window. In the morning, he shaved with icy water — more and more of his things were migrating from Malyshev Street — peering at himself in the speckled mirror. Then put on his shoes and left for work.

Lozovsky was mentioned only once in those weeks, when his wife suddenly said, 'Do you feel sorry for Mikhail?' They were in bed. It was early evening. It surprised him that she should mention her husband in such an offhand way. 'Yes,' he said.

'Why?'

'I liked him.'

'Did you?' She seemed surprised. 'Why?'

'Why these questions?'

'I just want to know.'

'I don't know why.'

Her next question, a minute or two later, was 'Did you like me the first time you saw me?'

'Yes.'

'When was the first time you saw me?'

It would have been the first night he spent at Metelyev Log. His memories of that night? His shoes were soaked through. The interior of the house smelled of wax polish, of kerosene — warm, oily smells. The milky hoods of the lamps looked like huge luminous mushrooms. The floor sounded hollow under his feet. However, he had no memory of *her* from that night.

'So you didn't like me the first time you saw me,' she said, with a laugh, when he told her this.

'I don't know. Maybe not the very first.'

'You liked me then though, when we met at Metelyev Log?'

'Yes.'

'You didn't seem to.' Though he was facing away from her, he was able to hear the smile in her voice. She put her hand forcefully through his hair and pulled it.

'Didn't I?'

'No, you didn't. You're very secretive, aren't you?'

He told her that when he got back from Metelyev Log, that first time, he had seen a Komsomol poster in Sverdlovsk station, a huge poster hanging half-hidden in darkness. It showed a rosy-cheeked young woman, wearing heavy workers' clothes, a mauve headscarf and an expression of exquisite stoicism as she trowelled mortar onto the brick that she was holding in her mittened hand. The woman in the poster looked quite like her, he said — more than that, there was about her a placid stillness very like the first, slightly misleading impression she herself had made on him (her china-blue eyes cow-like in their clouded placidity when she looked up from the page to see her husband and the Chekist enter the house) and he had fallen asleep that night thinking of her, and of the woman in the poster, the two of them merging together in his mind, so much so that when he next saw her, a few months later, he was surprised how different they were. She laughed. 'Were you disappointed?' she said.

Was he disappointed?

Perhaps 'disappointed' was too strong a word.

'No,' he said.

'I'm sure you were. And what about your wife?' she said. 'Did you like her the first time you saw her?'

He said he had no memory of the first time he had seen her. She would have been very young.

'How young?'

'Twelve, I suppose.'

'And how old were you?'

'Um . . . ' For a second he seemed not to understand the question. Then he said, 'The same age.'

20

One afternoon Mikhalkov summoned him to his office. Mikhalkov had started to smoke a pipe, a substantial black object. When Aleksandr sat down, it had extinguished itself, and he sat there waiting while Mikhalkov huffed and puffed and struck matches. 'Where have you been?' Mikhalkov said eventually, with his teeth on its stem. 'I've been trying to get hold of you all day.'

'I went to see Yudin.'

Mikhalkov himself had told him to do this.

'Oh yes? How is he?'

'He's the same. The same as he was.'

Puffing with the focused urgency of a doctor losing a patient, Mikhalkov said nothing for a few seconds. 'The same, eh?'

'Yes.'

'Oh well.'

That morning, more through luck than judgement — it was not easy to find people on those nameless tracks, in those unnumbered huts — he had found the place where Yudin lived with his mother. When he got out of the Pobeda, the stench was overpowering. There was an open sewer nearby. It was so sickening that he was tempted to hold his handkerchief over his nose. He did not. There were some people there, watching him. The wind fussed with various scraps of flapping jetsam, and tugged at some wire fencing with a monotonous tinging sound. The interior of the hut had its own unpleasant odour. Near the entrance was a space where newspapers were pinned on the wall, and there were some tattered books. Then the soiled sheets on strings and other makeshift partitions started — the hut was home to several dozen people, though in the middle of the day very few of them were there. Moving through these subdivisions, shoving them aside in light the colour of cobwebs, he stumbled on Yudin. For a second he was stunned — Yudin was sitting on the floor and seemed to be putting together some sort of small kerosene stove. 'He wants to help,' his mother said. 'When he's tried I'll do it.' And he saw that Yudin showed no sign of even knowing what the pieces of the stove were, and had no hope of successfully putting them together.

His mother was surprisingly old. She eyed Aleksandr suspiciously when he told her who he was. Her eyes were leathery slits, and she was smoking a sort of cheroot made of newspaper. Yudin smelled terrible — the filthy sour-milk smell of someone who has not undressed, let alone washed, for weeks.

'There's been,' Mikhalkov said, out of the side of his mouth, 'some news. Important. I'm telling everyone individually how it's going to affect them . . . '

Aleksandr was thinking of how, as he was leaving, Yudin's mother — proud, taciturn and mistrustful until then — suddenly seized his sleeve and said, 'Please, is there nowhere for him?'

'General Veklishev is leaving us,' Mikhalkov said. 'He's off to Moscow. A job at the ministry. A whole new world of shopping for *madame*. He's over the moon, but nervous. I've been asked to take over here.'

This was not surprising. It was well known that Veklishev was looking for a Moscow job, well known that Mikhalkov hoped to succeed him. Aleksandr said he was pleased for him — Mikhalkov smiled, and in his smile, which was warm, Aleksandr saw, not for the first time, the extent to which his suave superior thought him unworldly, even slightly simple. He knew that this was what Mikhalkov thought of him. He also knew that he liked him, that in unimportant ways he even looked up to him. So he was not surprised, either, when he said, 'I'm putting you in for promotion.'

'Thank you.'

Mikhalkov smiled once more, in the green upward illumination of his desk light. 'You did well with Lozovsky,' he said. 'It was a sensitive situation.'

He went to his office and lay on the chaise longue. He wondered what Mikhalkov had meant when he said, 'It was a sensitive situation.' He wished he had asked him. He had not wanted to seem naïve. Slowly the light faded, and lying there, hearing the natter of typewriters, he thought of Lozovsky, of the events leading up to his arrest, and of the part he had played in them.

His office was dark. Though it had been dark for some time, he had not switched on the electric light. When he finally stood up and did so, it was only to take his things and leave. For the first time in two weeks, he did not go to the flat on Karl Libknekht Street. He went home and slept on the divan. In fact he did not sleep much. In the morning he had to use Zalesky's razor, and when he had shaved, he sat for a long time on the divan, worrying a loose tile of parquet with the toe of his shoe. The room looked strange to him, stripped of Irina's things. He would be leaving it himself soon.

His promotion included new privileges, one of which was his own flat. There was a place on Studencheskaya Street, in a quiet suburb near the lake.

When he told her, later the same day, that he did not think they should see each other any more, first she just said, 'Okay,' as if it was a small thing. She seemed unsurprised. Then, for a long time, she was silent. On the table, still wrapped in tissue paper, was the dry-cleaning he had put there a few minutes earlier — some of her winter things that she had taken with her from Metelyev Log. She stared at it and smoothed the tissue paper with her fingers.

'I'm sorry,' he said.

She had been talking about his new flat. He had told her about it, and it seemed to be her assumption that she would move there with him. Things she said suggested this. For instance, she said she hoped there wouldn't be too many mosquitoes in the summer since they seemed to have 'a particular predilection' for her blood. It was when she said this that he had said, with what immediately seemed a savage lack of preamble, that he did not think they should see each other any more. She stood next to the table staring at the dry-cleaning. With a sort of shrug, as if it hurt her pride to say

230

it, she said, 'Why?'

He did not understand exactly why. Only years later did he see that it was from this that he found the strength, in 1960, to say that he did not think Lozovsky was innocent — from this sacrifice.

21

It is known as 'The Summit' — two superpowers, meeting on equal terms in the autumn of 1972 to thrash out their differences. The Soviet Union and Canada. Or to be precise, the ice-hockey teams of those two nations. The series started in Montreal, and from there proceeded to Toronto, then to Winnipeg. The fourth match was in Vancouver, where the Canadians were whistled off the ice by their own fans, the Soviets having won a second time to put themselves 2-1 up with the four Moscow meetings to follow. And when they won the first of those meetings, on 22 September, their opponents found themselves far from home, with food poisoning in a Soviet hotel, and seemingly facing defeat. They stopped eating in the hotel. Their food was flown in from Canada, and they took their meals at the Canadian embassy. Of the next two matches Tarasov said, 'They fought with the ferocity and intensity of trapped animals.' They levelled the series, with one match left to play.

That match is today. Aleksandr waits in the

twilight. When the series started, no one expected the Soviet Union to win a single match — if they succeeded in winning just one match it would be seen as a moral victory. The Canadians were professional sportsmen. The Soviets, steel workers and train drivers. So when the train drivers and steel workers won the first match in Montreal everyone was shocked — the players themselves seemed shocked that for long periods they had outplayed their opponents. And when the series moved to Moscow, with the steel workers and train drivers in the lead, some people started to think that they might even win it. Perhaps some people even started to think that they *would* win it. Aleksandr turns on the overhead light. Yes, perhaps some excitable people thought that it was more or less already won. And now? To lose now would be terrible. To lose when victory had seemed there for the taking.

It has started, and he turns up the volume. Within the first few minutes, Kompalla, the West German referee, penalises two of the Canadian players, and soon the horn sounds — with a two-man advantage the Soviets have scored. A minute later, Kompalla penalises another Canadian, who smashes his stick on the ice and yells foreign obscenities. When Kompalla increases the penalty, the Canadian makes to attack him with the stub of his stick. His teammates prevent him. The atmosphere is tense and ugly. The first period ends 2-2.

The Soviets score early in the second and, sensing a wavering of their opponents' self-belief, they attack implacably, trying to press home the win while they have the psychological upper hand. It seems to work. In the swish and smash of the event, they surge into a two-goal lead. And now, surely, it is time to start thinking of victory.

A minute into the final period the Canadians score. The next ten minutes seem to last an hour. The tension, the fear, are more intense than at any time in the entire series. Then the Canadians score again. One of their players smashes his way through the Soviet defence like a maniac. Tretiak saves, or so it seems for a fraction of a second, until a second Canadian slides in to whack home the puck. And then something happens. There is shouting. The horn has not sounded and the Canadian team staff are shouting at the match officials. The situation threatens to descend into a melee ... Aleksandr is suddenly aware of another voice mingling with the shouting from the radio, and Ozerov saying, '*I don't ... I don't know what's happening ...* ' Someone out in the street, shouting 'Uncle Sasha!' Standing impatiently, he throws open the window and looks out. '*I think the goal's been given*,' Ozerov is saying. His nephew, Andrey Ivanovich, is standing there in the damp darkness.

'Andryusha,' Aleksandr says, surprised. 'What is it?'

'My father's had a heart attack.'

Aleksandr says nothing.

'*Yes. It's been given. The score is 5-5 . . .* '

'I'm going to the hospital now,' Andrey says.

'I'll . . . I'll come with you.'

Without turning off the radio — '*Maltsev passes to Mikhailov, who skates forward . . .* ' — he fumbles on his overcoat and hat. Andrey was wearing neither — that was how he knew, as soon as he saw him, that something terrible had happened.

He is waiting at the wheel of his father's Lada. He looks like Ivan, and it is strange to see him there, sitting in that seat, smoking with such similar mannerisms. He shoves the engine into gear, however, with an unsolicitous violence that would make his father wince.

'What happened?' Aleksandr says.

'I don't know. I wasn't there. Agata phoned for the ambulance. And they took him to the Vilonov Street hospital! I said to her, 'Why didn't you tell them to take him to the Fourth

Department hospital?' They knew where he lived. What did they think?'

'How is he?'

'I don't know. I don't know.'

Andrey twists down the window and flicks his cigarette-end into the wind. He is forcing the Lada to travel at speed. The engine whines unhealthily.

'Is he . . . ? Will he . . . ?'

'Live? I don't know.'

Aleksandr has never seen his normally phlegmatic nephew so impassioned. He seems furious, on the point of lashing out. He has never got on well with his father. There is an ever-present tension, to do with the way that Ivan treated Katya, who now lives with Andrey and his wife.

Aleksandr himself feels nothing. He even finds himself wondering, with a sort of sad shame, who won the ice hockey. It will be over now. 'Where's Agata?' he says.

'She's at the hospital. I left her there. Why don't you have a phone?'

Andrey parks the Lada impatiently in front of the hospital and hurries inside, into the dingy light, the smell of disinfectant and under that the soup-kitchen smell, the wide humid hallways, the sinister quiet.

Agata is wearing a jacket seemingly made of gold sequins, and her face is thick with make-up that has smudged and spread with tears. Her eyes are pink, and she is holding a silk handkerchief. There is a young woman with her, a doctor. They are standing in a passageway next to a trolley on which a man is lying. His eyes are shut, his face grey and swollen. There is a transparent rubber oxygen mask strapped over his nose and mouth. His hair, Aleksandr thinks, looks very obviously dyed. To see him like that, Ivan does not seem the same person. So much so that Aleksandr almost expects to see him standing there with the others. That he is not there, nervously smoking, shocked like everyone else in this moment of family trauma, seems strange and terrible.

'What's happening?' Andrey says. 'How is he?'

The doctor looks at him sadly. 'He's okay.'

'Is he awake?'

'He's had a lot of morphine.'

Andrey says, 'I want him moved. He can't stay here.'

The doctor looks puzzled. 'Moved?' she says. 'Where?'

'To the Fourth Department hospital. I don't know why they brought him here . . . '

'We can't move him now.'

'Why not?'

'He's too weak.'

'What are you talking about?'

'He won't be able to move for days.'

'You said he was okay.'

'He is okay. But he's very weak . . . '

'Please, Andryusha,' Agata says.

'He shouldn't be here!' Andrey shouts. 'I want him moved.'

On the wall over the trolley on which Ivan is lying there is a picture, a page from a magazine that someone has put in a plastic frame. The picture is of a smiling little girl feeding a lamb from a horn. When he sees it, Aleksandr's eyes fill with tears and he lowers his head. Who did that? Who put that picture there? As if it had the slightest hope of offsetting the suffering to which it was witness every day. And yet why else would someone put it there? The innocence of this person, more than the innocence of the image itself, is what moves him. He snorts with emotion, inhales through his nostrils and looks up.

'I'm sorry, he is here — ' The doctor.

'And he shouldn't be! I want him moved!'

'Please don't shout.'

'Andryusha, please,' Agata's voice is pleading, tearful.

'I just told you — ' the doctor says.

'He shouldn't be here! Don't you understand that?'

Aleksandr stares sadly at Ivan's lifeless face under the transparent rubber of the oxygen mask. Agata has stopped pleading with Andrey. She weeps quietly, her handkerchief over her face, her shoulders shaking. Andrey insists on speaking to the senior doctor, who turns out to be a man in his fifties with hairy ears and a weighty, weary presence. Andrey speaks to him with strained politeness. 'My father was brought here by mistake,' he says. 'I want him moved to the Fourth Department hospital. That's where he should have been taken in the first place.'

'He's too weak to be moved,' the doctor says.

'How can he be too weak to be moved? He was moved here, wasn't he?'

'That was necessary.'

'And it's necessary to move him now.'

'No, it isn't — '

'Yes, it *is*!'

Aleksandr says, 'Andryusha . . .' and puts a hand on his arm. He throws it off. '*No!* What do you care?'

'What do I care? What do you mean? Andryusha!' With tears in his eyes, Andrey is leaving, walking quickly towards the lifts. 'Andryusha!' Aleksandr follows him for a few steps. The senior doctor sighs, and lights a cigarette. 'He's upset,' Aleksandr says.

'I know.'

'I'm sorry.'

'He can't be moved tonight. Or tomorrow.'

'I understand.'

'I might be able to find a room for him. Somewhere.'

'If it's possible . . . '

'We're very full at the moment.'

Agata has not been listening. Suddenly something in her seems to snap. As if in slow motion, she sinks to the red linoleum, sobbing violently. Her legs slide out in perpendicular directions. She starts to wail.

22

The next morning, Aleksandr finds her her normal self. Everything seems more normal, though it is the first time that he has seen her without make-up, and she looks older. Older than she is, in fact. Of course, she is exhausted. Her face is very pale, except for the semicircles under her eyes. She has almost no eyebrows, he notices; the way her hair is scraped back emphasises this. They are standing in the hallway, outside the small ward where space was found for Ivan. There is a window, slightly steamed up, with some pot plants on the sill.

She tells him matter-of-factly how she and Ivan were preparing to leave for a dinner party, Ivan was tying his tie and inspecting himself in the mirror when he started to sweat profusely. 'He was panting like a dog,' she says. He said he felt sick, and strange, and that he did not think he would be able to go to the party. He seemed very worried. And then suddenly he was in terrible pain. That was when she phoned for the ambulance. Everything happened so fast. She says that even then she thought how lucky it was that

Natalya, their four-year-old daughter, was not there. She was with Agata's parents for the evening.

While she waited for the ambulance, sitting tearfully on the floor in the hall next to her struggling husband — 'he was struggling like a fish out of water, exactly like that' — she phoned Andrey. The ambulance men, when they finally arrived, would not take her with them, so she had to wait for Andrey to drive her to the hospital. They went first to the Fourth Department hospital, but Ivan was not there, so they went to the hospital on Vilonov Street. 'I thought he would be dead by the time we got there,' she says.

Some yellow leaves still cling to the birches behind the hospital — yellow in the otherwise grey space of the hospital garden, where they are walking slowly on a cement path. 'The doctor says his heart might be damaged. And there's a chance he'll have another attack. Especially in the next few days. They say he can't have any physical or psychological stress. He can't have any visitors for now. I'm sorry you can't see him, Aleksandr Andreyevich.'

'I understand.'

'And he needs to stop smoking,' she says.

He holds open the door for her and they step inside, into the humid interior of the hospital. She has been there all night, is still wearing the same sparkly evening wear. The sequined jacket is on her shoulders like a shawl.

'I slept for a few hours,' she says, in the lift, when he asks her. 'On a sofa downstairs.'

'You should go home and sleep properly.'

'Andryusha will be here later. I'll go then.'

'Okay.'

Looking at her now, in the neon light of the lift, he feels that he has misjudged her in the past. In particular, he had not noticed, until now, how much she loves Ivan. He has never taken her, or their marriage, entirely seriously. She is his fourth wife, and was his secretary first, and is twenty years younger than he is. Aleksandr had always felt that she somehow tricked Ivan — foolish, sensuous, soft-hearted Ivan — into marrying her. Now it strikes him for the first time how much *she* puts up with. Ivan himself seems not to take her, or their marriage, entirely seriously. He is patronising to her, offhand, impatient, offensive — often in front of other people, in ways that seem intended to hurt and humiliate her.

'Andryusha says he's sorry,' she says.

'Sorry for what?'

'For what he said last night.'

'What did he say?'

'I don't know. He wouldn't tell me. He said

he said something to you.'

'Did he?'

'Yes.'

He shakes his head — pretends not to know what she means. However, he has been wondering ever since what his nephew meant when he said, *What do you care?* It stung him, no question. He wonders in particular what Ivan might have said to his son to prompt a question like that; wonders what sort of things are said about him in Ivan's family. It strikes him that if he had a family some fairly unpleasant things might sometimes be said, *en famille*, about Ivan.

'Well,' Agata says, 'he says he's sorry. He was upset.'

'I know.'

'Thank you for visiting, Aleksandr Andreyevich. I'm sorry you couldn't see him.' He is walking towards the lift when she says, 'Oh, Aleksandr Andreyevich?'

'Yes?'

'Would you mind stopping by our place and feeding Lovkach? That would be very helpful. The poor thing hasn't eaten since yesterday. I'd forgotten about him.' She starts searching through her handbag for the keys. 'Give him a tin of sardines — there's plenty there — and some milk.'

'Okay.'

'Leave the keys with Stepan. The porter,' she says.

'Okay.'

'Thank you.'

He waits for the tram on Mayakovsky Street. It is a sharp blue-skied September morning. This sort of autumn weather, these sort of mornings and their sad, still, quiet afternoons always make him think of the autumn of forty-eight, as if every autumn since then were only a memory of that one. The tram takes him to 1905 Square from where he walks the short distance to Ivan's flat. He is passing through the lobby when a voice shouts, 'Excuse me!' It is the porter, Stepan presumably, in his ill-fitting uniform. 'Who are you?' he says.

Aleksandr explains.

'Oh yes?' Stepan is openly sceptical. 'I don't know you.'

'No, you don't.'

'Well, they're not in,' he says.

'I know. I've got the key.'

'*Have* you?'

'My brother's in hospital. I'm here to feed the cat.'

For a moment Stepan squints at him suspiciously. Then — perhaps noticing that, despite his somewhat threadbare coat and very old astrakhan hat, his shoes are polished, his fingernails scrubbed — he seems to decide that what he has said is a plausible enough explanation for his presence. Certainly it would be a strange thing for an impostor to say. 'Eighth floor,' he murmurs, and Aleksandr summons the lift. It hums down, and stops with a loud tick.

The upstairs hall is silent. He lets himself into Ivan's flat. Lovkach — white, fluffy — is immediately there, miaowing loudly and showing his milky needle-teeth. He flicks his tail and trots up and down the parquet, shoving himself against the legs of the furniture. The hall is long and large, with the living room on the left. Part of the dividing wall is made of smoked glass and some shadowy daylight seeps through. Aleksandr shuts the front door and, with the usual slightly intrusive feeling of entering someone else's home when they are not there, followed by Lovkach, makes his way into the kitchen.

It is spotless and full of strange electric machines. The fridge is like a white sarcophagus. He takes out a plastic sack of milk and looks for a knife or scissors to open it with. There is a wooden block with several slots in it, in which knives of various sizes are inserted. He takes one of the smaller ones and saws at the plastic until it suddenly splits. Quite a lot of milk spills onto the floor, and

Lovkach starts to lick it up. Swearing quietly, Aleksandr fits the sack of milk into its special plastic holder and looks for something to pour some into. Then, while Lovkach laps noisily, he finds and opens a tin of sardines. He puts it on the floor next to what is left of the milk, and washes the oil from his hands.

While Lovkach eats, he wanders through the flat. On a table in the hall — over which hangs a deluxe portrait of Lenin under a picture light — there is some unopened mail, and invitations to official functions propped on the wall, and two tickets to the Sverdlovsk opera. Mozart's *Don Giovanni*. For tonight, he notices — Friday, 29 September 1972. (Ivan is no opera buff — it is the sort of thing that Agata would want to do.) There are framed photographs of Ivan's four children at various ages.

The living room is very large. Nevertheless, it is somewhat shadowy. The curtains are heavy green velvet. The furniture is sombre. From the far end, the fat television stares. There are shelves filled mostly with the works of Marx and Lenin in fine leather editions. There is an expensive Czech sound system, and some Western LPs, probably purchased in Yugoslavia. A malachite ashtray. Some journalism awards in frames on the wall. A black-and-white photo of Ivan meeting

Kosygin, part of a line-up of nervous provincial journalists, smiling and shaking his hand.

He slides open the terrace door and steps outside — the sharpness of the air is a shock after the well-heated flat. From the eighth floor, looking south-east, the low-lying city spreads out under white plumes of steam. The sky has a frosty shimmer. He looks for landmarks. Lenin Prospekt is an obvious one. And the lake, shining like polished metal — on the other side the park has turned yellow. The traffic noise is thin.

23

The Fourth Department hospital, once the suburban villa of a Yekaterinburg industrialist, is surrounded by a high wall. The wall is old now, buckling in places, flaking, eaten by damp, discoloured. Over the brown barbed wire that spirals along its summit are the bare branches of mature trees. A young soldier — a teenager with a shadow moustache — stands at the gate, holding a machine gun in his mittened hands as if he is not sure what it is. He looks worried when Aleksandr walks up to him. Few people arrive here on foot — there are ambulances, long Zil limousines, minibuses full of staff. Solitary people who have walked from the tram stop on Volgograd Street, however, are seldom seen. When Aleksandr says who he is, the soldier withdraws into his tar-paper hut and, eyeing his elderly visitor suspiciously through its scuffed plastic window, picks up the phone. It is a dull October afternoon.

The exterior of the hospital is shabby, the paintwork falling off in stiff pieces. Not so the interior. Polished parquet floors, a faintly medicinal smell, the quiet of a university library. In the foyer, Aleksandr unwinds his scarf and takes off his astrakhan hat. It is old now, its elegantly shiny surface losing its profound lustre, starting to separate into stiff individual hairs; its satin lining fraying to show the simple felt underneath. It was a present from Irina. Her last to him, for his birthday in February forty-eight.

Ivan is sitting up in bed, propped on a pile of pillows, surrounded by newspaper pages and sweet wrappers. He is holding a newspaper, and peering at it through heavy-framed spectacles. The radio is on — a serious female voice, the news — and Aleksandr Ivanovich sits easily in a velvet armchair, still in his soft overcoat, trying successfully to impress his father by translating the German text on the packaging of some pharmaceuticals. They both turn to the door when Aleksandr enters.

'Sasha!' Ivan says, whipping off the large spectacles and slipping them into the breast pocket of his pyjamas. Aleksandr Ivanovich puts down the West German medicine and smiles, though without warmth. He leaves soon afterwards. 'See you tomorrow, Dad,' he says, leaning over to kiss Ivan.

'Yes, see you tomorrow, Shurik.'

When he has left, however, Ivan says, 'I won't see him tomorrow, of course.'

'Oh? Why not?' And then, when Ivan says nothing, 'It's tomorrow, is it?'

'Tonight.'

'Well, you'll see him the day after then. How long is he here for?'

'In Sverdlovsk? I don't know.'

'And Galina?'

'Yes, she was here this morning.' Ivan sighs. 'She brought me that. Very kind of her.'

There is a trug of fruit, including a small fresh pineapple, on a side table.

'I'm not allowed to smoke,' Ivan says, unwrapping a sweet, while Aleksandr studies the spiky-topped fruit. Though he has tasted it in tins, in its natural state it is something new to him. 'You're not allowed to smoke?' he says. 'That's not surprising.'

'I eat these to try and take my mind off it, but it doesn't work.'

Aleksandr puts down the pineapple. 'How are you feeling?' he says.

'Okay. Fine, actually.'

'You look well.'

'Do I?'

'Yes.'

In fact Ivan looks puffy and his face has a suffocated purplish hue; even speaking seems to leave him slightly short-winded. 'I feel fine,' he says. 'And I tell them that. I tell them.'

There is a small possibility that he will not survive the operation. The doctors are quite open about it. They say that without it another heart attack is almost inevitable. For the last few weeks, he has been totally sedentary, has slept with an oxygen mask strapped to his face; it has left a stipple of irritation around his mouth. He picks up one of the newspapers that surround him, and then immediately puts it down. 'How are you?' he says.

Aleksandr shrugs.

On the radio, the serious woman says that, following the signing of the US-Soviet trade pact on 18 October, Armand Hammer, the president of the Occidental Petroleum Corporation, is in Moscow. Sounding very slightly proud, she says that Mr Hammer has presented the Soviet Union with a Goya painting 'worth one million dollars'. Negotiations on a trade package will start imminently, and will be finalised, it is hoped, in time for Brezhnev's visit to the United States in the spring of 1973 . . .

'Do you mind if I turn it off?'

'No.' In his nest of newspapers, Ivan shakes his head, his thoughts elsewhere. 'No.' Aleksandr turns off the radio, and in the sudden silence sits down on the velvet armchair. They talk for a while.

When he leaves it is late afternoon. The old stairs squeak under his feet in the oak-panelled stairwell. Outside wet snow is starting to fall. It forms a thin slush on the dark tarmac of the drive, settles frailly on the sombre cedars that surround the hospital. A light is on in the soldier's hut. It is a long walk to the tram stop. And then, in this suburb, he might have to wait forty minutes for a tram.

24

He married again in 1960, twelve years after
he and Irina were divorced — Serafima, a
KGB colleague, a small, softly spoken
woman, whose first husband was a war hero
who died at Stalingrad. 1960 was the time of
his troubles with the Lozovsky case — the
tribunal — and she was strongly opposed to
his treatment. Politically, they were on the
same side. It was the functional marriage of
two people in their late forties, without too
many illusions left, and the divorce, in 1964,
was perfectly friendly. For a few years, he still
saw her quite often. He never saw Irina in the
same way. She moved to Moscow, where one
of her younger sisters was married to
someone important. Sometime in the late
sixties she must have moved back to
Sverdlovsk — one day he saw her in the park
near 1905 Square, feeding the pigeons. He
had not seen her for twenty years, not even at
Nikita Stepanovich's funeral.

He was sitting on a bench under the trees
— it was his lunch hour — when he noticed
the middle-aged woman feeding the pigeons.
Though it was summer, she was wearing a

grey raincoat, and her hair was grey, and every few moments she put her hand into the plastic bag she was holding and threw more crumbs to the pigeons. Filthy and flapping, they entirely surrounded her. It was only when she turned to leave that he saw her face, and then only for a second. He watched her walk away. She still walked the way she used to. When she was almost out of sight, he stood up and started to follow her. She was some way ahead, and in the sunlight of Lenin Prospekt she quickened her pace. Still in the shade of the park he tried to do the same. He would not have been able to whisper her name, much less shout it out. There was a tram standing at the stop. That was why she had started to jog. The doors shut, she hit them and they opened again. The tram moved off. He stood on the pavement of Lenin Prospekt, frighteningly light-headed. The sun was in his face. He did not feel well.

Someone even said, 'You alright?'

Was he alright?

'Yes,' he said. 'Yes, thank you.'

'What?'

He shook his head.

'You should sit down.'

He nodded, and let them lead him to a bench in the shade.

Several people were looking down at him.

One of them was holding his hat, which he must have dropped. 'My hat,' he said. It was handed to him. He put it on. 'Thank you.' He smiled. He was embarrassed to find himself in this situation. His shirt was wet. 'I'm fine,' he said, still smiling. 'Thank you.' They looked sceptical, but when he stood up — standing made his head spin — they stood aside to let him leave.

She died of lung cancer in 1971. He did not find out until the spring of the following year.

Acknowledgements

I am particularly indebted to the work of three historians. Sheila Fitzpatrick's *Everyday Stalinism*; Stephen Kotkin's *Magnetic Mountain: Stalinism as a Civilisation*; and Jochen Hellbeck's *Revolution on my Mind: Writing a Diary under Stalin*, especially the chapters on Stepan Podlubnyi and Zinaida Denisevskaya. Other books that were useful to me were: *Russia: the People and the Power* by Robert G. Kaiser; *The Road to Terror: Stalin and the Self-Destruction of the Bolsheviks, 1932–1939* by J. Arch Getty and Oleg V. Naumov; *Stalin's Secret Pogrom: The Postwar Inquisition of the Jewish Anti-Fascist Committee* by Joshua Rubenstein and Vladimir P. Naumov; *Stalinism as a Way of Life* by Lewis Siegelbaum and Andrei Sokolov; *Soviet Workers and Late Stalinism* by Donald Filtzer; *The Great Urals: Regionalism and the Evolution of the Soviet System* by James R. Harris; *Cold Peace: Stalin and the Soviet Ruling Circle, 1945–1953* by Yoram Gorlizki and Oleg Khlevniuk; *Khrushchev Remembers* by Nikita Khrushchev; *Stalin, The Court of the Red Tsar* by Simon Sebag Montefiore; and finally, though it was in fact the starting point of the whole thing, *The Man with a Shattered World* by A. R. Luria.

I would also like to thank my agent, Anna Webber, and Dan Franklin and Alex Bowler at Jonathan Cape, for all their input and support.